Books by Ernest Hemingway

ACROSS THE RIVER
AND INTO THE TREES

ACROSS THE RIVER

AND

INTO THE TREES

BY

ERNEST HEMINGWAY

CHARLES   SCRIBNER'S   SONS

NEW   YORK

To Mary With Love

ACROSS THE RIVER
AND INTO THE TREES

CHAPTER I

THEY started two hours before daylight, and at first, it was not necessary to break the ice across the canal as other boats had gone on ahead. In each boat, in the darkness, so you could not see, but only hear him, the poler stood in the stern, with his long oar. The shooter sat on a shooting stool fastened to the top of a box that contained his lunch and shells, and the shooter's two, or more, guns were propped against the load of wooden decoys. Somewhere, in each boat, there was a sack with one or two live mallard hens, or a hen and a drake, and in each boat there was a dog who shifted and shivered uneasily at the sound of the wings of the ducks that passed overhead in the darkness.

Four of the boats went on up the main canal toward the big lagoon to the north. A fifth boat had already turned off into a side canal. Now, the sixth boat turned south into a shallow lagoon, and there was no broken water.

It was all ice, new-frozen during the sudden, windless cold of the night. It was rubbery and bending against the thrust of the boatman's oar. Then it would break as sharply as a pane of glass, but the boat made little forward progress.

"Give me an oar," the shooter in the sixth boat said. He stood up and braced himself carefully. He could hear the ducks passing in the darkness, and feel the restless lurching of the dog. To the north he heard the sound of breaking ice from the other boats.

"Be careful," the poler in the stern said. "Don't tip the boat over."

"I am a boatman, too," the shooter said.

He took the long oar the boatman handed him and reversed it so he could hold it by the blade. Holding the blade he reached forward and punched the handle through the ice. He felt the firm bottom of the shallow lagoon, put his weight on the top of the wide oar-blade, and holding with both hands and, first pulling, then shoving, until the pole-hold was well to the stern, he drove the boat ahead to break the ice. The ice broke like sheets of plate glass as the boat drove into it, and onto it, and astern the boatman shoved them ahead into the broken passage.

After a while, the shooter, who was working hard and steadily and sweating in his heavy clothes, asked the boatman, "Where is the shooting barrel?"

"Off there to the left. In the middle of the next bay."

"Should I turn for it now?"

"As you wish."

"What do you mean, as I wish? You know the water. Is there water to carry us there?"

"The tide is low. Who knows?"

"It will be daylight before we get there if we don't hurry."

The boatman did not answer.

All right, you surly jerk, the shooter thought to himself. We are going to get there. We've made two-thirds of the way now and if you are worried about having to work to break ice to pick up birds, that is altogether too bad.

"Get your back in it, jerk," he said in English.

"What?" the boatman asked in Italian.

"I said let's go. It's going to be light."

It was daylight before they reached the oaken staved hogshead sunk in the bottom of the lagoon. It was surrounded by a sloping rim of earth that had been planted with sedge and grass, and the shooter swung carefully up onto this, feeling the frozen grasses break as he stepped on them. The boatman lifted the combination shooting stool and shell box out of the boat and handed it to the shooter, who leaned over and placed it in the bottom of the big barrel.

The shooter, wearing his hip boots and an old combat jacket, with a patch on the left shoulder that no one understood, and with the slight light places on the straps, where stars had been removed, climbed down into the barrel and the boatman handed him his two guns.

He placed them against the wall of the barrel and hung

his other shell bag between them, hanging it on two hooks built into the wall of the sunken barrel. Then he leaned the guns against each side of the shell bag.

"Is there water?" he asked the boatman.

"No water," the boatman said.

"Can you drink the lagoon water?"

"No. It is unhealthy."

The shooter was thirsty from the hard work of breaking the ice and driving the boat in and he felt his anger rise, and then held it, and said, "Can I help you in the boat to break ice to put out the decoys?"

"No," the boatman said and shoved the boat savagely out onto the thin sheet ice that cracked and ripped as the boat drove up onto it. The boatman commenced smashing at the ice with the blade of his oar and then started tossing decoys out to the side and behind him.

He's in a beautiful mood, the shooter thought. He's a big brute, too. I worked like a horse coming out here. He just pulled his weight and that's all. What the hell is eating him? This is his trade, isn't it?

He arranged the shooting stool so he would have the maximum swing to left and right, opened a box of shells, and filled his pockets and opened another of the boxes of shells in the shell bag so he could reach into it easily. In front of him, where the lagoon lay glazed in the first light, was the black boat and the tall, heavily built boatman smashing with his oar at the ice and tossing decoys overboard as though he were ridding himself of something obscene.

It was getting lighter now and the shooter could see the low line of the near point across the lagoon. Beyond that point he knew there were two other shooting posts and far beyond it there was more marsh and then the open sea. He loaded both his guns and checked the position of the boat that was putting out decoys.

From behind him, he heard the incoming whisper of wings and he crouched, took hold of his right hand gun with his right hand as he looked up from under the rim of the barrel, then stood to shoot at the two ducks that were dropping down, their wings set to brake, coming down dark in the gray dim sky, slanting toward the decoys.

His head low, he swung the gun on a long slant, down, well and ahead of the second duck, then without looking at the result of his shot he raised the gun smoothly, up, up ahead and to the left of the other duck that was climbing to the left and as he pulled, saw it fold in flight and drop among the decoys in the broken ice. He looked to his right and saw the first duck a black patch on the same ice. He knew he had shot carefully on the first duck, far to the right of where the boat was, and on the second, high out and to the left, letting the duck climb far up and to the left to be sure the boat was out of any line of fire. It was a lovely double, shot exactly as he should have shot, with complete consideration and respect for the position of the boat, and he felt very good as he reloaded.

"Listen," the man in the boat called. "Don't shoot toward the boat."

I'll be a sad son of a bitch, the shooter said to himself. I will indeed.

"Get your decoys out," he called to the man in the boat. "But get them out fast. I won't shoot until they are all out. Except straight overhead."

The man in the boat said nothing that could be heard.

I can't figure it, the shooter thought to himself. He knows the game. He knows I split the work, or more, coming out. I never shot a safer or more careful duck in my life than that. What's the matter with him? I offered to put the dekes out with him. The hell with him.

Out on the right now, the boatman was still chopping angrily at the ice, and tossing out the wooden decoys in a hatred that showed in every move he made.

Don't let him spoil it, the shooter told himself. There won't be much shooting with this ice unless the sun should melt it later on. You probably will only have a few birds, so don't let him spoil it for you. You don't know how many more times you will shoot ducks and do not let anything spoil it for you.

He watched the sky lightening beyond the long point of marsh, and turning in the sunken barrel, he looked out across the frozen lagoon, and the marsh, and saw the snow-covered mountains a long way off. Low as he was, no foot-hills showed, and the mountains rose abruptly from the plain. As he looked toward the mountains he could feel a breeze on his face and he knew, then, the wind would come from there, rising with the sun, and that some birds

6

would surely come flying in from the sea when the wind disturbed them.

The boatman had finished putting out the decoys. They were in two bunches, one straight ahead and to the left toward where the sun would rise, and the other to the shooter's right. Now he dropped over the hen mallard with her string and anchor, and the calling duck bobbed her head under water, and raising and dipping her head, splashed water onto her back.

"Don't you think it would be good to break more ice around the edges?" the shooter called to the boatman. "There's not much water to attract them."

The boatman said nothing but commenced to smash at the jagged perimeter of ice with his oar. This ice breaking was unnecessary and the boatman knew it. But the shooter did not know it and he thought, I do not understand him but I must not let him ruin it. I must keep it entire and not let him do it. Every time you shoot now can be the last shoot and no stupid son of a bitch should be allowed to ruin it. Keep your temper, boy, he told himself.

CHAPTER II

BUT he was not a boy. He was fifty and a Colonel of
Infantry in the Army of the United States and to pass
a physical examination that he had to take the day before he
came down to Venice for this shoot, he had taken enough
mannitol hexanitrate to, well he did not quite know what
to—to pass, he said to himself.

The surgeon had been quite skeptical. But he noted the
readings after taking them twice.

"You know, Dick," he said. "It isn't indicated; in fact
it is definitely contra-indicated in increased intra-ocular
and intra-cranial pressure."

"I don't know what you are talking about," the shooter,
who was not a shooter, then, except potentially, and was a
Colonel of Infantry in the Army of the United States,
reduced from being a general officer, said.

"I have known you a long time, Colonel. Or maybe it
just seems a long time," the surgeon told him.

"It's been a long time," the Colonel said.

"We sound like song writers," the surgeon said. "But don't you ever run into anything, or let any sparks strike you, when you're really souped up on nitroglycerin. They ought to make you drag a chain like a high-octane truck.

"Wasn't my cardiograph O.K.?" the Colonel asked.

"Your cardiograph was wonderful, Colonel. It could have been that of a man of twenty-five. It might have been that of a boy of nineteen."

"Then what are you talking about?" the Colonel asked.

That much mannitol hexanitrate produced a certain amount of nausea, sometimes, and he was anxious for the interview to terminate. He was also anxious to lie down and take a seconal. I ought to write the manual of minor tactics for the heavy pressure platoon, he thought. Wish I could tell him that. Why don't I just throw myself on the mercy of the court? You never do, he told himself. You always plead them non-guilty.

"How many times have you been hit in the head?" the surgeon asked him.

"You know," the Colonel told him. "It's in my 201."

"How many times have you been hit *on* the head?"

"Oh Christ." Then he said. "You are asking for the army or as my physician?"

"As your physician. You didn't think I'd try to wind your clock, did you?"

"No, Wes. I'm sorry. Just what was it you wanted to know?"

"Concussions."

"Real ones?"

"Any time you were cold or couldn't remember afterwards."

"Maybe ten," the Colonel said. "Counting polo. Give or take three."

"You poor old son of a bitch," the surgeon said. "Colonel, sir," he added.

"Can I go now?" the Colonel asked.

"Yes, sir," the surgeon said. "You're in good shape."

"Thanks," the Colonel said. "Want to go on a duck shoot down in the marshes at the mouth of the Tagliamento? Wonderful shoot. Some nice Italian kids I met up at Cortina own it."

"Is that where they shoot coots?"

"No. They shoot real ducks at this one. Good kids. Good shoot. Real ducks. Mallard, pin-tail, widgeon. Some geese. Just as good as at home when we were kids."

"I was kids in twenty-nine and thirty."

"That's the first mean thing I ever heard you say."

"I didn't mean it like that. I just meant I didn't remember when duck shooting was good. I'm a city boy, too."

"That's the only God-damn trouble with you, too. I never saw a city boy yet that was worth a damn."

"You don't mean that, do you, Colonel?"

"Of course, not. You know damn well I don't."

"You're in good shape, Colonel," the surgeon said. "I'm sorry I can't go on the shoot. I can't even shoot."

"Hell," said the Colonel. "That doesn't make any difference. Neither can anybody else in this army. I'd like to have you around."

"I'll give you something else to back up what you're using."

"Is there anything?"

"Not really. They're working on stuff, though."

"Let 'em work," the Colonel said.

"I think that's a laudable attitude, sir."

"Go to hell," the Colonel said. "You sure you don't want to go?"

"I get my ducks at Longchamps on Madison Avenue," the surgeon said. "It's air-conditioned in the summer and it's warm in the winter and I don't have to get up before first light and wear long-horned underwear."

"All right, City Boy. You'll never know."

"I never wanted to know," the surgeon said. "You're in good shape, Colonel, sir."

"Thanks," said the Colonel and went out.

CHAPTER III

THAT was day before yesterday. Yesterday he had driven down from Trieste to Venice along the old road that ran from Monfalcone to Latisana and across the flat country. He had a good driver and he relaxed completely in the front seat of the car and looked out at all this country he had known when he was a boy.

It looks quite differently now, he thought. I suppose it is because the distances are all changed. Everything is much smaller when you are older. Then, too, the roads are better now and there is no dust. The only times I used to ride through it was in a camion. The rest of the times we walked. I suppose what I looked for then, was patches of shade when we fell out, and wells in farm yards. And ditches, too, he thought. I certainly looked for plenty of ditches.

They made a curve and crossed the Tagliamento on a temporary bridge. It was green along the banks and men were fishing along the far shore where it ran deep. The blown bridge was being repaired with a snarl of riveting hammers, and eight hundred yards away the smashed buildings and outbuildings of what was now a ruined country house once built by Longhena showed where the mediums had dropped their loads.

"Look at it," the driver said. "In this country you find a bridge or a railway station. Then go half a mile from it in any direction and you find it like that."

"I guess the lesson is," the Colonel said, "don't ever build yourself a country house, or a church, or hire Giotto to paint you any frescoes, if you've got a church, eight hundred yards away from any bridge."

"I knew there must be a lesson in it, sir," the driver said.

They were past the ruined villa now and onto the straight road with the willows growing by the ditches still dark with winter, and the fields full of mulberry trees. Ahead a man was pedalling a bicycle and using both his hands to read a paper.

"If there are heavies the lesson ought to say a mile," the driver said. "Would that be about right, sir?"

"If it's guided missiles," the Colonel said. "Better make it two hundred and fifty miles. Better give that cyclist some horn."

The driver did, and the man moved over to the side of the road without either looking up or touching his handle-bars. As they passed him, the Colonel tried to see what paper he was reading, but it was folded over.

"I guess a man would do better now not to build himself a fine house or a church, or to get who did you say it was to paint frescoes?"

"Giotto, I said. But it could be Piero della Francesca or Mantegna. Could be Michelangelo."

"Do you know a lot about painters, sir?" the driver asked.

They were on a straight stretch of road now and were making time so that one farm blended, almost blurred, into another farm and you could only see what was far ahead and moving toward you. Lateral vision was just a condensation of flat, low country in the winter. I'm not sure I like speed, the Colonel thought. Brueghel would have been in a hell of a shape if he had to look at the country like this.

"Painters?" he answered the driver. "I know quite a little about them, Burnham."

"I'm Jackson, sir. Burnham's up at the rest center at Cortina. That's a fine place, sir."

"I'm getting stupid," the Colonel said. "Excuse me, Jackson. It is a fine place. Good chow. Well run. Nobody bothers you."

"Yes, sir," Jackson agreed. "Now the reason I asked you about painters, is these madonnas. I thought I ought to see some painting so I went to that big place in Florence."

"The Uffizi? The Pitti?"

"Whatever they call it. The biggest one. And I kept looking at those paintings until madonnas started to run out of my ears. I tell you, Colonel, sir, a man who hasn't been checked out on this painting can only see just about so many madonnas and it gets him. You know my theory? You know how crazy they are about bambinis and the less they got to eat the more bambinis they got and that they have coming? Well, I think these painters were probably big bambini lovers like all Italians. I don't know these ones you mentioned just now, so I don't include them in my theory and you'll put me straight anyway. But it looks to me like these madonnas, that I really saw plenty of, sir, it looks to me like these just straight ordinary madonna painters were sort of a manifest, say, of this whole bambini business, if you understand what I mean."

"Plus the fact that they were restricted to religious subjects."

"Yes, sir. Then you think there is something to my theory?"

"Sure. I think it is a little more complicated, though."

"Naturally, sir. It's just my preliminary theory."

"Do you have any other theories on art, Jackson?"

"No, sir. That bambini theory is as far as I've thought it through. What I wish is, though, they would paint some good pictures of that high country up around the rest center at Cortina."

"Titian came from up there," the Colonel said. "At least they say he did. I went down the valley and saw the house where he was supposed to be born."

"Was it much of a place, sir?"

"Not so much."

"Well, if he painted any pictures of that country up

around there, with those sunset color rocks and the pines and the snow and all the pointed steeples—"

"*Campaniles*," the Colonel said. "Like that one ahead at Ceggia. It means bell tower."

"Well, if he painted any really good pictures of that country I'd sure as hell like to trade him out of some of them."

"He painted some wonderful women," the Colonel said.

"If I had a joint or a roadhouse or some sort of an inn, say, I could use one of those," the driver said. "But if I brought home a picture of some woman, my old woman would run me from Rawlins to Buffalo. I'd be lucky if I *got* to Buffalo."

"You could give it to the local museum."

"All they got in the local museum is arrow heads, war bonnets, scalping knives, different scalps, petrified fish, pipes of peace, photographs of Liver Eating Johnston, and the skin of some bad man that they hanged him and some doctor skinned him out. One of those women pictures would be out of place there."

"See that next *campanile* down there across the plain?" the Colonel said. "I'll show you a place down there where we used to fight when I was a kid."

"Did you fight here, too, sir?"

"Yeah," the Colonel said.

"Who had Trieste in that war?"

"The Krauts. The Austrians, I mean."

"Did we ever get it?"

"Not till the end when it was over."

"Who had Florence and Rome?"

"We did."

"Well, I guess you weren't so damned bad off then."

"Sir," the Colonel said gently.

"I'm sorry, sir," the driver said quickly. "I was in the Thirty-Sixth Division, sir."

"I've seen the patch."

"I was thinking about the Rapido, sir, I didn't mean to be insolent or lacking in respect."

"You weren't," the Colonel said. "You were just thinking about the Rapido. Listen, Jackson, everybody who's soldiered a long time has had their Rapidos and more than one."

"I couldn't take more than one, sir."

The car went through the cheerful town of San Dona di Piave. It was built up and new, but no more ugly than a middle western town, and it was as prosperous and as cheery as Fossalta, just up the river, is miserable and gloomy, the Colonel thought. Did Fossalta never get over the first war? I never saw it before it was smacked, he thought. They shelled it badly before the big fifteenth of June offensive in eighteen. Then we shelled it really badly before we retook it. He remembered how the attack had taken off from Monastier, gone through Fornace, and on this winter day he remembered how it had been that summer.

A few weeks ago he had gone through Fossalta and had gone out along the sunken road to find the place where he had been hit, out on the river bank. It was easy to find because of the bend of the river, and where the heavy machine gun post had been, the crater was smoothly grassed. It had been cropped, by sheep or goats, until it looked like a designed depression in a golf course. The river was slow and a muddy blue here, with reeds along the edges, and the Colonel, no one being in sight, squatted low, and looking across the river from the bank where you could never show your head in daylight, relieved himself in the exact place where he had determined, by triangulation, that he had been badly wounded thirty years before.

"A poor effort," he said aloud to the river and the river bank that were heavy with autumn quiet and wet from the fall rains. "But my own."

He stood up and looked around. There was no one in sight and he had left the car down the sunken road in front of the last and saddest rebuilt house in Fossalta.

"Now I'll complete the monument," he said to no one but the dead, and he took an old Sollingen clasp knife such as German poachers carry, from his pocket. It locked on opening and, twirling it, he dug a neat hole in the moist earth. He cleaned the knife on his right combat boot and then inserted a brown ten thousand lira note in the hole and tamped it down and put the grass that he had cored out, over it.

"That is twenty years at 500 lira a year for the Medaglia d'Argento al Valore Militare. The V.C. carries ten guineas, I believe. The D.S.C. is non-productive. The Silver Star is free. I'll keep the change," he said.

It's fine now, he thought. It has merde, money, blood;

look how that grass grows; and the iron's in the earth along with Gino's leg, both of Randolfo's legs, and my right kneecap. It's a wonderful monument. It has everything. Fertility, money, blood and iron. Sounds like a nation. Where fertility, money, blood and iron is, there is the fatherland. We need coal though. We ought to get some coal.

Then he looked across the river to the rebuilt white house that had once been rubble, and he spat in the river. It was a long spit and he just made it.

"I couldn't spit that night nor afterwards for a long time," he said. "But I spit good now for a man who doesn't chew."

He walked slowly back to where the car was parked. The driver was asleep.

"Wake up, son," he had said. "Turn her around and take that road toward Treviso. We don't need a map on this part. I'll give you the turns."

CHAPTER IV

NOW, on his way into Venice, keeping strictly controlled and unthinking his great need to be there, the
big Buick cleared the last of San Dona and came up onto the
bridge over the Piave.

They crossed the bridge and were on the Italian side of
the river and he saw the old sunken road again. It was as
smooth and undistinguished now, as it was all along the
river. But he could see the old positions. And now, along
each side of the straight, flat, canal-bordered road they
were making time on, were the willows of the two canals
that had contained the dead. There had been a great killing
at the last of the offensive and someone, to clear the river
bank positions and the road in the hot weather, had ordered
the dead thrown into the canals. Unfortunately, the canal
gates were still in the Austrians' hands down the river,
and they were closed.

So there was little movement to the water, and the dead
had stayed there a long time, floating and bloating face up
and face down regardless of nationality until they had

attained colossal proportions. Finally, after organization had been established, labor troops hauled them out at night and buried them close to the road. The Colonel looked for added greenness close to the road but could not note any. However, there were many ducks and geese in the canals, and men were fishing in them all along the road.

They dug them all up anyway, the Colonel thought, and buried them in that big *ossario* up by Nervesa.

"We fought along here when I was a kid," the Colonel told the driver.

"It's a God-damn flat country to fight in," the driver said. "Did you hold that river?"

"Yes," the Colonel said. "We held it and lost it and took it back again."

"There isn't a contour here as far as you can see."

"That was the trouble," the Colonel said. "You had to use contours you couldn't see, they were so small, and ditches and houses and canal banks and hedgerows. It was like Normandy only flatter. I think it must have been something like fighting in Holland."

"That river sure doesn't look anything like the Rapido."

"It was a pretty good old river," the Colonel said. "Up above, it had plenty of water then, before all these hydro-electric projects. And it had very deep and tricky channels in the pebbles and shingle when it was shallow. There was a place called the Grave di Papadopoli where it was plenty tricky."

He knew how boring any man's war is to any other man, and he stopped talking about it. They always take it personally, he thought. No one is interested in it, abstractly, except soldiers and there are not many soldiers. You make them and the good ones are killed, and above they are always bucking for something so hard they never look or listen. They are always thinking of what they have seen and while you are talking they are thinking of what they will say and what it may lead to in their advancement or their privilege. There was no sense boring this boy, who, for all his combat infantryman badge, his Purple Heart and the other things he wore, was in no sense a soldier but only a man placed, against his will, in uniform, who had elected to remain in the army for his own ends.

"What did you do in civil life, Jackson?" he asked.

"I was partners with my brother in a garage in Rawlins, Wyoming, sir."

"Are you going back there?"

"My brother got killed in the Pacific and the guy who was running the garage was no good," the driver said. "We lost what we had put in it."

"That's bad," the Colonel said.

"You're God-damned right it's bad," the driver said and added, "sir."

The Colonel looked up the road.

He knew that if they kept on this road they would come, shortly, to the turn that he was waiting for; but he was impatient.

"Keep your eyes open and take a left hand turn on the road leading off this pike," he told the driver.

"Do you think those low roads will be good with this big car, sir?"

"We'll see," the Colonel said. "Hell, man, it hasn't rained in three weeks."

"I don't trust those side roads in this low country."

"If we get stuck, I'll haul you out with oxen."

"I was only thinking about the car, sir."

"Well, think about what I told you and turn off on the first left side road you see if it looks practicable."

"That looks like one coming up, from the hedges," the driver said.

"You're all clear behind. Pull up just ahead of it and I'll go over and have a look."

He stepped out of the car and walked across the wide, hard-surfaced road and looked at the narrow dirt road, with the swift flowing canal beside it, and the thick hedge beyond. Beyond the hedge, he saw a low red farmhouse with a big barn. The road was dry. There were not even cart ruts sunk in it. He got back into the car.

"It's a boulevard," he said. "Quit worrying."

"Yes, sir. It's your car, sir."

"I know," the Colonel said. "I'm still paying for it. Say, Jackson, do you always suffer so much any time you go off a highway onto a secondary road?"

"No, sir. But there's a lot of difference between a jeep, and a car as low hung as this. Do you know the clearance you have on your differential and your body frame on this?"

"I've got a shovel in the trunk and we've got chains. Wait till you see where we're going after we leave Venice."

"Do we go all the way in this car?"

"I don't know. I'll see."

"Think about your fenders, sir."

"We'll cut the fenders off like the Indians do in Oklahoma. She's over-fendered right now. She's got too much of everything except engine. Jackson, that's a real engine she's got. One hundred and fifty ponies."

"It certainly is, sir. It's a great pleasure to drive that big engine on the good roads. That's why I don't want anything to happen to her."

"That's very good of you, Jackson. Now just quit suffering."

"I'm not suffering, sir."

"Good," said the Colonel.

He was not, either, because just then he saw, beyond the line of close-bunched brown trees ahead, a sail moving along. It was a big red sail, raked sharply down from the peak, and it moved slowly behind the trees.

Why should it always move your heart to see a sail moving along through the country, the Colonel thought. Why does it move my heart to see the great, slow, pale oxen? It must be the gait as well as the look of them and the size and the color.

But a good fine big mule, or a string of pack mules in good condition, moves me, too. So does a coyote every time I ever see one, and a wolf, gaited like no other animal, gray and sure of himself, carrying that heavy head and with the hostile eyes.

"Ever see any wolves out around Rawlins, Jackson?"

"No, sir. Wolves were gone before my time; they poisoned them out. Plenty coyotes, though."

24

"Do you like coyotes?"

"I like to hear them nights."

"So do I. Better than anything, except seeing a ship sailing along through the country."

"There's a boat doing that over there, sir."

"On the Sile canal," the Colonel told him. "She's a sailing barge going to Venice. This wind is off the mountains now and she makes it along pretty good. It's liable to turn really cold tonight if this wind holds and it ought to bring in plenty ducks. Turn to your left here and we'll run along the canal. There's a good road."

"They didn't have much duck shooting where I came from. But there was plenty of it in Nebraska along the Platte."

"Do you want to shoot where we're going?"

"I don't believe so, sir. I'm not much of a shot, and I'd rather stay in that sack. It's a Sunday morning, you know."

"I know," the Colonel said. "You can stay in the sack until noon if you want."

"I brought my repellent. I ought to sleep O.K."

"I'm not sure you'll need it," the Colonel said. "Did you bring any K-rations or Ten in One? They're liable to eat Italian food, you know."

"I brought a few cans to help out and a little stuff to give away."

"That's good," the Colonel said.

He was looking ahead now to see where the canal road joined the main highway again. There he knew that he would see it on a clear day such as this was. Across the marshes, brown as those at the mouths of the Mississippi around Pilot Town are in winter, and with their reeds bent by the heavy north wind, he saw the squared tower of the church at Torcello and the high *campanile* of Burano beyond it. The sea was a slate blue and he could see the sails of twelve sailing barges running with the wind for Venice.

I'll have to wait until we cross the Dese River above Noghera to see it perfectly, he thought. It is strange to remember how we fought back there along the canal that winter to defend it and we never saw it. Then one time, I was back as far as Noghera and it was clear and cold like today, and I saw it across the water. But I never got into it. It is my city, though, because I fought for it when I was a boy, and now that I am half a hundred years old, they know I fought for it and am a part owner and they treat me well.

Do you think that's why they treat you well, he asked himself.

Maybe, he thought. Maybe they treat me well because I'm a chicken colonel on the winning side. I don't believe it, though. I hope not, anyway. It is not France, he thought.

There you fight your way into a city that you love and are very careful about breaking anything and then, if you have good sense, you are careful not to go back because you will meet some military characters who will resent your having fought your way in. *Vive la France et les pommes de terre frites. Liberté, Venalité, et Stupidité.* The great *clarté* of the French military thinking. They haven't had a military thinker since du Picq. He was a poor bloody Colonel, too. *Mangin, Maginot* and *Gamelin.* Take your choice, Gentlemen. Three schools of thought. One; I hit them on the nose. Two; I hide behind this thing which does not cover my left flank. Three; I hide my head in the sand like an ostrich, confident in the greatness of France as a military power and then take off.

Take off is putting it very cleanly and pleasantly. Sure, he thought, whenever you over-simplify you become unjust. Remember all the fine ones in the Resistance, remember Foch both fought and organized and remember how fine the people were. Remember your good friends and remember your deads. Remember plenty things and your best friends again and the finest people that you know. Don't be a bitter nor a stupid. And what has that to do with soldiering as a trade? Cut it out, he told himself. You're on a trip to have fun.

"Jackson," he said, "are you happy?"

"Yes, sir."

"Good. Shortly, we are coming to a view that I want you to see. You only have to take one look at it. The entire operation will be practically painless."

I wonder what he's riding me for now, the driver thought. Just because he was a B.G. once he knows everything. If he was any good as a B.G. why didn't he hold it? He's been beat up so much he's slug-nutty.

"There's the view, Jackson," the Colonel said. "Stop her by the side of the road and we'll take a look."

The Colonel and the driver walked over to the Venice

side of the road and looked across the lagoon that was
whipped by the strong, cold wind from the mountains that
sharpened all the outlines of buildings so that they were
geometrically clear.

"That's Torcello directly opposite us," the Colonel
pointed. "That's where the people lived that were driven
off the mainland by the Visigoths. They built that church
you see there with the square tower. There were thirty
thousand people lived there once and they built that church
to honor their Lord and to worship him. Then, after they
built it, the mouth of the Sile River silted up or a big flood
changed it, and all that land we came through just now
got flooded and started to breed mosquitoes and malaria hit
them. They all started to die, so the elders got together and
decided they should pull out to a healthy place that would
be defensible with boats, and where the Visigoths and the
Lombards and the other bandits couldn't get at them,
because these bandits had no sea-power. The Torcello
boys were all great boatmen. So they took the stones of all
their houses in barges, like that one we just saw, and they
built Venice."

He stopped. "Am I boring you, Jackson?"

"No, sir. I had no idea who pioneered Venice."

"It was the boys from Torcello. They were very tough
and they had very good taste in building. They came from
a little place up the coast called Caorle. But they drew on all
the people from the towns and the farms behind when the
Visigoths over-ran them. It was a Torcello boy who was
running arms into Alexandria, who located the body of

St. Mark and smuggled it out under a load of fresh pork so the infidel customs guards wouldn't check him. This boy brought the remains of St. Mark to Venice, and he's their patron saint and they have a cathedral there to him. But by that time, they were trading so far to the east that the architecture is pretty Byzantine for my taste. They never built any better than at the start there in Torcello. That's Torcello there."

It was, indeed.

"St. Mark's square is where the pigeons are and where they have that big cathedral that looks sort of like a moving picture palace, isn't it?"

"Right, Jackson. You're on the ball. If that's the way you look at it. Now you look beyond Torcello you will see the lovely *campanile* on Burano that has damn near as much list on it as the leaning tower of Pisa. That Burano is a very over-populated little island where the women make wonderful lace, and the men make bambinis and work day-times in the glass factories in that next island you see on beyond with the other *campanile*, which is Murano. They make wonderful glass day-times for the rich of all the world, and then they come home on the little vaporetto and make bambinis. Not everyone passes every night with his wife though. They hunt ducks nights too, with big punt guns, out along the edge of the marshes on this lagoon you're looking across now. All night long on a moonlight night you hear the shots." He paused.

"Now when you look past Murano you see Venice. That's my town. There's plenty more I could show you, but I think we probably ought to roll now. But take one good look at it. This is where you can see how it all happened. But nobody ever looks at it from here."

"It's a beautiful view. Thank you, sir."

"O.K.," the Colonel said. "Let's roll."

CHAPTER V

BUT he continued to look and it was all as wonderful to him and it moved him as it had when he was eighteen years old and had seen it first, understanding nothing of it and only knowing that it was beautiful. The winter had come very cold that year and all the mountains were white beyond the plain. It was necessary for the Austrians to try to break through at the angle where the Sile River and the old bed of the Piave were the only lines of defense.

If you had the old bed of the Piave then you had the Sile to fall back on if the first line did not hold. Beyond the Sile there was nothing but bare-assed plain and a good road network into the Veneto plain and the plains of Lombardy, and the Austrians attacked again and again and again late through the winter, to try to get onto this fine road that they were rolling on now which led straight to Venice. That winter the Colonel, who was a lieutenant then, and in a foreign army, which had always made him slightly suspect afterwards in his own army, and had done his career no good, had a sore throat all winter. This sore throat was from being in the water so much. You could not get dry and it was better to get wet quickly and stay wet.

The Austrian attacks were ill-coordinated, but they were constant and exasperated and you first had the heavy bombardment which was supposed to put you out of business, and then, when it lifted, you checked your positions and counted the people. But you had no time to care for wounded, since you knew that the attack was coming immediately, and then you killed the men who came wading across the marshes, holding their rifles above the water and coming as slow as men wade, waist deep.

If they did not lift the shelling when it started, the Colonel, then a lieutenant, often thought, I do not know what we would be able to do. But they always lifted it and moved it back ahead of the attack. They went by the book.

If we had lost the old Piave and were on the Sile they would move it back to the second and third lines; although such lines were quite untenable, and they should have brought all their guns up very close and whammed it in all the time they attacked and until they breached us. But thank God, some high fool always controls it, the Colonel thought, and they did it piecemeal.

All that winter, with a bad sore throat, he had killed men who came, wearing the stick bombs hooked up on a harness under their shoulders with the heavy, calf hide packs and the bucket helmets. They were the enemy.

But he never hated them; nor could have any feeling about them. He commanded with an old sock around his throat, which had been dipped in turpentine, and they broke down the attacks with rifle fire and with the machine guns which still existed, or were usable, after the bombardment. He taught his people to shoot, really, which is a rare ability in continental troops, and to be able to look at the enemy when they came, and, because there was always a dead moment when the shooting was free, they became very good at it.

But you always had to count and count fast after the bombardment to know how many shooters you would have. He was hit three times that winter, but they were all gift wounds; small wounds in the flesh of the body without breaking bone, and he had become quite confident of his personal immortality since he knew he should have been killed in the heavy artillery bombardment that always preceded the attacks. Finally he did get hit properly and for good. No one of his other wounds had ever done to him what the first big one did. I suppose it is just the loss of the immortality, he thought. Well, in a way, that is quite a lot to lose.

This country meant very much to him, more than he could, or would ever tell anyone and now he sat in the car happy that in another half hour they would be in Venice. He took two mannitol hexanitrate tablets; since he had always been able to spit since 1918, he could take them dry, and asked,

"How are you doing, Jackson?"

"Fine, sir."

"Take the left outside road when we hit the fork for Mestre and we'll be able to see the boats along the canal and miss that main traffic."

"Yes, sir," the driver said. "Will you check me on the fork?"

"Of course," the Colonel said.

They were coming up on Mestre fast, and already it was like going to New York the first time you were ever there in the old days when it was shining, white and beautiful. I stole that, he thought. But that was before the smoke. We are coming into my town, he thought. Christ, what a lovely town.

They made the left turn and came along the canal where the fishing boats tied up, and the Colonel looked at them and his heart was happy because of the brown nets and the wicker fish traps and the clean, beautiful lines of the boats. It's not that they are picturesque. The hell with picturesque. They are just damned beautiful.

They passed the long line of boats in the slow canal that carried water from the Brenta, and he thought about the long stretch of the Brenta where the great villas were, with their lawns and their gardens and the plane trees and the cypresses. I'd like to be buried out there, he thought. I know the place very well. I don't believe you could fix it, though. I don't know. I know some people that might let me be buried on their place. I'll ask Alberto. He might think it was morbid, though.

For a long time he had been thinking about all the fine

places he would like to be buried and what parts of the earth he would like to be a part of. The stinking, putrefying part doesn't last very long, really, he thought, and anyway you are just a sort of mulch, and even the bones will be some use finally. I'd like to be buried way out at the edge of the grounds, but in sight of the old graceful house and the tall, great trees. I don't think it would be much of a nuisance to them. I could be a part of the ground where the children play in the evenings, and in the mornings, maybe, they would still be training jumping horses and their hoofs would make the thudding on the turf, and trout would rise in the pool when there was a hatch of fly.

They were up on the causeway from Mestre to Venice now with the ugly Breda works that might have been Hammond, Indiana.

"What do they make there, sir?" Jackson asked.

"The company makes locomotives in Milan," the Colonel said. "Here they make a little of everything in the metallurgic line."

It was a miserable view of Venice now and he always disliked this causeway except that you made such good time and you could see the buoys and the channels.

"This town makes a living on its own," he said to Jackson. "She used to be the queen of the seas and the people are very tough and they give less of a good God-damn about things than almost anybody you'll ever meet. It's a tougher town than Cheyenne when you really know it, and everybody is very polite."

"I wouldn't say Cheyenne was a tough town, sir."

"Well, it's a tougher town than Casper."

"Do you think that's a tough town, sir?"

"It's an oil town. It's a nice town."

"But I don't think it's tough, sir. Or ever was."

"O.K., Jackson. Maybe we move in different circles. Or maybe we have a differing definition for the word. But this town of Venice, with everybody being polite and having good manners, is as tough as Cooke City, Montana, on the day they have the Old Timers' Fish Fry."

"My idea of a tough town is Memphis."

"Not like Chicago, Jackson. Memphis is only tough if you are a Negro. Chicago is tough North, South, there isn't any East, and West. But nobody has any manners. But in this country, if you ever want to know a *really* tough town where they eat wonderfully too, go to Bologna."

"I never was there."

"Well, there's the Fiat garage where we leave the car," the Colonel said. "You can leave the key at the office. They don't steal. I'll go in the bar while you park upstairs. They have people that will bring the bags."

"Is it okay to leave your gun and shooting gear in the trunk, sir?"

"Sure. They don't steal here. I told you that once."

"I wanted to take the necessary precaution, sir, on your valuable property."

"You're so damned noble that sometimes you stink," the Colonel said. "Get the wax out of your ears and hear what I say the first time."

"I heard you, sir," Jackson said. The Colonel looked at him contemplatively and with the old deadliness.

He sure is a mean son of a bitch, Jackson thought, and he can be so God-damn nice.

"Get my and your bag out and park her up there and check your oil, your water and your tires," the Colonel said, and walked across the oil and rubber stained cement of the entry of the bar.

CHAPTER VI

IN THE bar, sitting at the first table as he came in, there was a post-war rich from Milan, fat and hard as only Milanese can be, sitting with his expensive looking and extremely desirable mistress. They were drinking *negronis*, a combination of two sweet vermouths and seltzer water, and the Colonel wondered how much taxes the man had escaped to buy that sleek girl in her long mink coat and the convertible he had seen the chauffeur take up the long, winding ramp, to lock away. The pair stared at him with the bad manners of their kind and he saluted, lightly, and said to them in Italian, "I am sorry that I am in uniform. But it is a uniform. Not a costume."

Then he turned his back on them, without waiting to see the effect of his remark, and walked to the bar. From the bar you could watch your luggage, just as well as the two *pescecani* were watching theirs.

He is probably a Commendatore, he thought. She is a

beautiful, hard piece of work. She is damned beautiful, actually. I wonder what it would have been like if I had ever had the money to buy me that kind and put them into the mink? I'll settle for what I have, he thought, and they can go and hang themselves.

The bar-tender shook hands with him. This bar-tender was an Anarchist but he did not mind the Colonel being a Colonel at all. He was delighted by it and proud and loving about it as though the Anarchists had a Colonel, too, and in some ways, in the several months that they had known each other, he seemed to feel that he had invented, or at least, erected the Colonel as you might be happy about participating in the erection of a *campanile*, or even the old church at Torcello.

The bar-tender had heard the conversation, or, rather, the flat statement at the table and he was very happy.

He had already sent down, via the dumb-waiter, for a Gordon's gin and Campari and he said, "It is coming up in that hand-pulled device. How does everything go at Trieste?"

"About as you would imagine."

"I couldn't even imagine."

"Then don't strain," the Colonel said, "and you will never get piles."

"I wouldn't mind it if I was a Colonel."

"I never mind it."

"You'd be over-run like a dose of salts," the waiter said.

"Don't tell the Honorable Pacciardi," the Colonel said.

He and the bar-tender had a joke about this because the

Honorable Pacciardi was Minister of Defense in the Italian Republic. He was the same age as the Colonel and had fought very well in the first world war, and had also fought in Spain as a battalion Commander where the Colonel had known him when he, himself, was an observer. The seriousness with which the Honorable Pacciardi took the post of Minister of Defense of an indefensible country was a bond between the Colonel and the bar-tender. The two of them were quite practical men and the vision of the Honorable Pacciardi defending the Italian Republic stimulated their minds.

"It's sort of funny up there," the Colonel said, "and I don't mind it."

"We must mechanize the Honorable Pacciardi," the bar-tender said. "And supply him with the atomic bomb."

"I've got three of them in the back of the car," the Colonel said. "The new model, complete with handles. But we can't leave him unarmed. We must supply him with botulism and anthrax."

"We cannot fail the Honorable Pacciardi," the bar-tender said. "Better to live one day as a lion than a hundred years as a sheep."

"Better to die on our feet than to live on our knees," the Colonel said. "Though you better get on your belly damn fast if you want to stay alive in plenty places."

"Colonel, do not say anything subversive."

"We will strangle them with our bare hands," the Colonel said. "A million men will spring to arms overnight."

"Whose arms?" the bar-tender asked.

"All that will be attended to," the Colonel said. "It's only a phase in the Big Picture."

Just then the driver came in the door. The Colonel saw that while they had been joking, he had not watched the door and he was annoyed, always, with any lapse of vigilance or of security.

"What the hell's been keeping you, Jackson? Have a drink."

"No, thank you, sir."

You prissy jerk, the Colonel thought. But I better stop riding him, he corrected.

"We'll be going in a minute," the Colonel said. "I've been trying to learn Italian from my friend here." He turned to look at the Milan profiteers; but they were gone.

I'm getting awfully slow, he thought. Somebody will take me any day now. Maybe even the Honorable Pacciardi, he thought.

"How much do I owe you?" he asked the bar-tender shortly.

The bar-tender told him and looked at him with his wise Italian eyes, not merry now, although the lines of merriment were clearly cut where they radiated from the corners of each eye. I hope there is nothing wrong with him, the bar-tender thought. I hope to God, or anything else, there's nothing really bad.

"Good-bye, my Colonel," he said.

"*Ciao*," the Colonel said. "Jackson, we are going down the long ramp and due north from the exit to where the

41

small launches are moored. The varnished ones. There is a porter with the two bags. It is necessary to let them carry them since they have a concession."

"Yes, sir," said Jackson.

The two of them went out the door and no one looked back at anyone.

At the *imbarcadero*, the Colonel tipped the man who had carried their two bags and then looked around for a boatman he knew.

He did not recognize the man in the launch that was first on call, but the boatman said, "Good-day, my Colonel. I'm the first."

"How much is it to the Gritti?"

"You know as well as I, my Colonel. We do not bargain. We have a fixed tariff."

"What's the tariff?"

"Three thousand five hundred."

"We could go on the vaporetto for sixty."

"And nothing prevents you going," the boatman, who was an elderly man with a red but un-choleric face, said. "They won't take you to the Gritti but they will stop at the imbarcadero past Harry's, and you can telephone for someone from the Gritti to get your bags."

And what would I buy with the God-damn three thousand five hundred lire; and this is a good old man.

"Do you want me to send that man there?" he pointed to a destroyed old man who did odd jobs and ran errands around the docks, always ready with the un-needed aid to the elbow of the ascending or descending passenger, always ready to help when no help was needed, his old felt hat held out as he bowed after the un-needed act. "He'll take you to the vaporetto. There's one in twenty minutes."

"The hell with it," the Colonel said. "Take us to the Gritti."

"*Con piacere*," the boatman said.

The Colonel and Jackson lowered themselves into the launch which looked like a speed boat. It was radiantly varnished and lovingly kept and was powered with a marine conversion of a tiny Fiat engine that had served its allotted time in the car of a provincial doctor and had been purchased out of one of the grave-yards of automobiles, those mechanical elephant cemeteries that are the one certain thing you may find in our world near any populated center, and been reconditioned and reconverted to start this new life on the canals of this city.

"How is the motor doing?" the Colonel asked. He could hear her sounding like a stricken tank or T.D., except the noises were in miniature from the lack of power.

"So-so," the boatman said. He moved his free hand in a parallel motion.

"You ought to get the smallest model Universal puts out. That's the best and lightest small marine engine I know."

"Yes," the boatman said. "There are quite a few things I should get."

"Maybe you'll have a good year."

"It's always possible. Lots of *pescecani* come down from Milano to gamble at the Lido. But nobody would ride twice in this thing on purpose. As a boat, it is fine, too. It is a well built, pleasant boat. Not beautiful as a gondola is, of course. But it needs an engine."

"I might get you a jeep engine. One that was condemned and you could work it over."

"Don't talk about such things," the boatman said. "Things like that don't happen. I don't want to think about it."

"You can think about it," the Colonel said. "I'm talking true."

"You mean it."

"Sure. I don't guarantee anything. I'll see what I can do. How many children have you got?"

"Six. Two male and four female."

"Hell, you mustn't have believed in the Regime. Only six."

"I *didn't* believe in the Regime."

"You don't have to give me that stuff," the Colonel said. "It would have been quite natural for you to *have* believed in it. Do you think I hold that against a man after we've won?"

They were through the dull part of the canal that runs from Piazzale Roma to Ca'Foscari, though none of it is dull, the Colonel thought.

It doesn't all have to be palaces nor churches. Certainly that isn't dull. He looked to the right, the starboard, he thought. I'm on the water. It was a long low pleasant building and there was a trattoria next to it.

I ought to live here. On retirement pay I could make it all right. No Gritti Palace. A room in a house like that and

44

the tides and the boats going by. I could read in the mornings and walk around town before lunch and go every day to see the Tintorettos at the Accademia and to the Scuola San Rocco and eat in good cheap joints behind the market, or, maybe, the woman that ran the house would cook in the evenings.

I think it would be better to have lunch out and get some exercise walking. It's a good town to walk in. I guess the best, probably. I never walked in it that it wasn't fun. I could learn it really well, he thought, and then I'd have that.

It's a strange, tricky town and to walk from any part to any other given part of it is better than working cross-word puzzles. It's one of the few things to our credit that we never smacked it, and to *their* credit that they respected it.

Christ, I love it, he said, and I'm so happy I helped defend it when I was a punk kid, and with an insufficient command of the language and I never even saw her until that clear day in the winter when I went back to have that small wound dressed, and saw her rising from the sea. Merde, he thought, we did very well that winter up at the juncture.

I wish I could fight it again, he thought. Knowing what I know now and having what we have now. But they'd have it too and the essential problem is just the same, except who holds the air.

And all this time he had been watching the bow of the beat-up beautifully varnished, delicately brass-striped boat, with the brass all beautifully polished, cut the brown water, and seen the small traffic problems.

They went under the white bridge and under the un-
finished wood bridge. Then they left the red bridge on the
right and passed under the first high-flying white bridge.
Then there was the black iron fret-work bridge on the
canal leading into the Rio Nuovo and they passed the
two stakes chained together but not touching: like us the
Colonel thought. He watched the tide pull at them and he
saw how the chains had worn the wood since he first had
seen them. That's us, he thought. That's our monument.
And how many monuments are there to us in the canals of
this town?

Then they still went slowly until the great lantern that
was on the right of the entrance to the Grand Canal where
the engine commenced its metallic agony that produced a
slight increase in speed.

Now they came down and under the Accademia between the pilings where they passed, at touching distance,
a heavily loaded black, diesel boat full of cut timber, cut
in chunks, to burn for firewood in the damp houses of the
Sea City.

"That's beech, isn't it?" the Colonel asked the boatman.

"Beech and another wood that is cheaper that I do not
recall, at this moment, the name of."

"Beech is, to an open fire, as anthracite coal is to a stove.
Where do they cut that beech?"

"I'm not a man of the mountains. But I think it comes
from up beyond Bassano on the other side of the Grappa.
I went there to the Grappa to see where my brother was
buried. It was an excursion that they made from Bassano,

and we went to the big ossario. But we returned by Feltre. I could see it was a fine timber country on the other side as you came down the mountains into the valley. We came down that military road, and they were hauling lots of wood."

"In what year was your brother killed on Grappa?"

"In nineteen-eighteen. He was a patriot and inflamed by hearing d'Annunzio talk, and he volunteered before his class was called. We never knew him very well because he went so quickly."

"How many were you in the family?"

"We were six. We lost two beyond the Isonzo, one on the Bainsizza and one on the Carso. Then we lost this brother I speak of on the Grappa and I remained."

"I'll get you the God-damned jeep complete with handles," the Colonel said. "Now let's not be morbid and look for all the places where my friends live."

They were moving up the Grand Canal now and it was easy to see where your friends lived.

"That's the house of the Contessa Dandolo," the Colonel said.

He did not say, but thought, she is over eighty, and she is as gay as a girl and does not have any fear of dying. She dyes her hair red and it looks very well. She is a good companion and an admirable woman.

Her *palazzo* was pleasant looking, set well back from the Canal with a garden in front and a landing place of its own where many gondolas had come, in their various times, bringing hearty, cheerful, sad and disillusioned people. But most of them had been cheerful because they were going to see the Contessa Dandolo.

Now, beating up the Canal, against the cold wind off the mountains, and with the houses as clear and sharp as on a winter day, which, of course, it was, they saw the old magic of the city and its beauty. But it was conditioned, for the Colonel, by his knowing many of the people who lived in the palazzos; or if no one lived there now, knowing to what use the different places had been put.

There's Alvarito's mother's house, he thought, and did not say.

She never lives there much and stays out at the country house near Treviso where they have trees. She's tired of there not being trees in Venice. She lost a fine man and nothing really interests her now except efficiency.

But the family at one time lent the house to George Gordon, Lord Byron, and nobody sleeps now in Byron's bed nor in the other bed, two flights below, where he used to sleep with the gondolier's wife. They are not sacred, nor relics. They are just extra beds that were not used afterwards for various reasons, or possibly to respect Lord Byron who was well loved in this town, in spite of all the errors he committed. You have to be a tough boy in this town to be loved, the Colonel thought. They never cared anything for Robert Browning, nor Mrs. Robert Browning, nor for their dog. They weren't Venetians no matter how well he wrote of it. And what is a tough boy, he asked himself. You use it so loosely you should be able to define it. I suppose it is a man who will make his play and then

48

backs it up. Or just a man who backs his play. And I'm not thinking of the theatre, he thought. Lovely as the theatre can be.

And yet, he thought, seeing now the little villa, close up against the water, ugly as a building you would see on the boat train from Havre or Cherbourg, coming into the banlieue before Paris as you came into town. It was over-run with badly administered trees, and not a place that you would live in if you could help it. There *he* lived.

They loved him for his talent, and because he was bad, and he was brave. A Jewish boy with nothing, he stormed the country with his talent, and his rhetoric. He was a more miserable character than any that I know and as mean. But the man I think of to compare him with never put the chips on the line and went to war, the Colonel thought, and Gabriele d'Annunzio (I always wondered what his real name was, he thought, because nobody is named d'Annunzio in a practical country and perhaps he was not Jewish and what difference did it make if he was or was not,) had moved through the different arms of the service as he had moved into and out of the arms of different women.

All the arms were pleasant that d'Annunzio served with and the mission was fast and easily over, except the Infantry. He remembered how d'Annunzio had lost an eye in a crash, flying as an observer, over Trieste or Pola, and how, afterwards, he had always worn a patch over it and people who did not know, for, then, no one really knew, thought it had been shot out at the Veliki or San Michele or some other bad place beyond the Carso where everyone died, or was incapacitated, that you knew. But d'Annunzio, truly, was only making heroic gestures with the other things. An Infantryman knows a strange trade, he thought; perhaps the strangest. He, Gabriele, flew, but he was not a flier. He was in the Infantry but he was not an Infantry-man and it was always the same appearances.

And the Colonel remembered one time when he had stood, commanding a platoon of assault troops, while it was raining in one of the interminable winters, when the rain fell always; or at least, always when there were parades or speeches to the troops, and d'Annunzio, with his lost eye, covered by the patch, and his white face, as white as the belly of a sole, new turned over in the market, the brown side not showing, and looking thirty hours dead, was shouting, "Morire non è basta," and the Colonel, then a lieutenant, had thought, "What the muck more do they want of us?"

But he had followed the discourse and, at the end, when the Lieutenant Colonel d'Annunzio, writer and national hero, certified and true if you must have heroes, and the Colonel did not believe in heroes, asked for a moment of silence for our glorious dead, he had stood stiffly at atten-tion. But his platoon, who had not followed the speech, there being no loud speakers then, and they being slightly out of hearing of the orator, responded, as one man, at the pause for the moment of silence for our glorious dead, with a solid and ringing *"Evviva d'Annunzio."*

They had been addressed before by d'Annunzio after victories, and before defeats, and they knew what they should shout if there was any pause by an orator.

The Colonel, being then a lieutenant, and loving his platoon, had joined with them and uttered, with the tone of command, *"Evviva d'Annunzio,"* thus absolving all those who had not listened to the discourse, speech, or harangue, and attempting, in the small way a lieutenant can attempt anything, except to hold an indefensible position, or intelligently direct his own part in an attack, to share their guilt.

But now he was passing the house where the poor beat-up old boy had lived with his great, sad, and never properly loved actress, and he thought of her wonderful hands, and her so transformable face, that was not beautiful, but that gave you all love, glory, and delight and sadness; and of the way the curve of her fore-arm could break your heart, and he thought, Christ they are dead and I do not know where either one is buried even. But I certainly hope they had fun in that house.

"Jackson," he said, "that small villa on the left belonged to Gabriele d'Annunzio, who was a great writer."

"Yes, sir," said Jackson, "I'm glad to know about him. I never heard of him."

"I'll check you out on what he wrote if you ever want to read him," the Colonel said. "There are some fair English translations."

"Thank you, sir," said Jackson. "I'd like to read him anytime I have time. He has a nice practical looking place. What did you say the name was?"

"D'Annunzio," the Colonel said. "Writer."

He added to himself, not wishing to confuse Jackson, nor be difficult, as he had been with the man several times that day, writer, poet, national hero, phraser of the dialectic of

Fascism, macabre egotist, aviator, commander, or rider, in the first of the fast torpedo attack boats, Lieutenant Colonel of Infantry without knowing how to command a company, nor a platoon properly, the great, lovely writer of *Notturno* whom we respect, and jerk.

Up ahead now there was a crossing place of gondolas at the Santa Maria del Giglio and, beyond, was the wooden dock of the Gritti.

"That's the hotel where we are stopping at, Jackson."

The Colonel indicated the three story, rose colored, small, pleasant palace abutting on the Canal. It had been a dependence of the Grand Hotel—but now it was its own hotel and a very good one. It was probably the best hotel, if you did not wish to be fawned on, or fussed over, or over-flunkied, in a city of great hotels, and the Colonel loved it.

"It looks O.K. to me, sir," Jackson said.

"It is O.K.," the Colonel said.

The motor boat came gallantly up beside the piling of the dock. Every move she makes, the Colonel thought, is a triumph of the gallantry of the aging machine. We do not have war horses now like old Traveller, or Marbot's Lysette who fought, personally, at Eylau. We have the gallantry of worn-through rods that refuse to break; the cylinder head that does not blow though it has every right to, and the rest of it.

"We're at the dock, sir," Jackson said.

"Where the hell else would we be, man. Jump out while I settle with this sportsman."

He turned to the boatman and said, "That was thirty five hundred, wasn't it?"

"Yes, my Colonel."

"I'll not forget about the over-age jeep engine. Take this and buy your horse some oats."

The porter, who was taking the bags from Jackson, heard this and laughed.

"No veterinarian will ever fix his horse."

"She still runs," the boatman said.

"But she doesn't win any races," the porter said. "How are you, my Colonel?"

"I couldn't be better," the Colonel said. "How are all the members of the Order?"

"All members are well."

"Good," said the Colonel. "I will go in and see the Grand Master."

"He is waiting for you, my Colonel."

"Let us not keep him waiting, Jackson," the Colonel said. "You may proceed to the lobby with this gentleman and tell them to sign me in. See the sergeant gets a room," he said to the porter. "We're here for the night only."

"The Baron Alvarito was here looking for you."

"I'll find him at Harry's."

"Good, my Colonel."

"Where is the Grand Master?"

"I'll find him for you."

"Tell him I'll be in the bar."

CHAPTER VII

THE bar was just across from the lobby of the Gritti, although lobby, the Colonel thought, was not the accurate term to describe that gracious entrance. Didn't Giotto describe a circle, he thought? No, that was in math. What he remembered and loved best as an anecdote about that painter was: "It was easy," said Giotto as he drew the perfect circle. Who the hell had said that and where?

"Good evening, Privy Counsellor," he said to the barman, who was not a full paid-up member of the order but whom he did not wish to offend. "What can I do for you?"

"Drink, my Colonel."

The Colonel looked out of the windows and the door of the bar onto the waters of the Grand Canal. He could see the big black hitching post for the gondolas and the late afternoon winter light on the wind-swept water. Across the Canal was the old Palace and a wood barge, black and broad, was coming up the Canal, her bluff bows pushing up a wave even though she had the wind behind her.

"Make it a very dry Martini," the Colonel said. "A double."

Just then the Grand Master came into the room. He was wearing his formal attire as a head waiter. He was truly handsome as a man should be, from the inside out, so that his smile starts from his heart, or whatever is the center of the body, and comes frankly and beautifully to the surface, which is the face.

He had a fine face with the long, straight nose of his part of the Veneto; the kind, gay, truthful eyes and the honorable white hair of his age, which was two years older than that of the Colonel.

He advanced smiling, lovingly, and yet conspiratorially, since they both shared many secrets, and he extended his hand, which was a big, long, strong, spatular fingered hand; well kept as was becoming, as well as necessary, to his position, and the Colonel extended his own hand, which had been shot through twice, and was slightly misshapen. Thus contact was made between two old inhabitants of the Veneto, both men, and brothers in their membership in the human race, the only club that either one paid dues to, and brothers, too, in their love of an old country, much fought over, and always triumphant in defeat, which they had both defended in their youth.

Their handshake was only long enough to feel, firmly, the contact and the pleasure of meeting and then the *Maitre d'Hotel* said, "My Colonel."

The Colonel said, "*Gran Maestro.*"

Then the Colonel asked the *Gran Maestro* to accompany him in a drink, but the *Maitre d'Hotel* said that he was working. It was impossible as well as forbidden.

"Fornicate forbidden," said the Colonel.

"Of course," the *Gran Maestro* said. "But everyone must comply with his duty, and here the rules are reasonable, and we all should comply with them; me especially, as a matter of precept."

"Not for nothing are you the *Gran Maestro,*" the Colonel said.

"Give me a small *Carpano punto e mezzo,*" the *Gran Maestro* said to the bar-tender, who was still outside of the Order for some small, not defined, un-stated reason. "To drink to the *ordine.*"

Thus, violating orders and the principle of precept and example in command, the Colonel and the *Gran Maestro* downed a quick one. They did not hurry nor did the *Gran Maestro* worry. They simply made it fast.

"Now, let us discuss the affairs of the Order," the Colonel said. "Are we in the secret chamber?"

"We are," said the *Gran Maestro.* "Or I declare it to be such."

"Continue," said the Colonel.

The order, which was a purely fictitious organization, had been founded in a series of conversations between the *Gran Maestro* and the Colonel. Its name was *El Ordine Militar, Nobile y Espirituoso de los Caballeros de Brusadelli.* The Colonel and the head waiter both spoke Spanish, and since that is the best language for founding orders, they had used it in the naming of this one, which was named after a particularly notorious multi-millionaire non-taxpaying profiteer of Milan, who had, in the course of a dispute over property, accused his young wife, publicly and legally through due process of law, of having deprived him of his judgment through her extraordinary sexual demands.

"*Gran Maestro*," the Colonel said. "Have you heard from our Leader, *The Revered One?*"

"Not a word. He is silent these days."

"He must be thinking."

"He must."

"Perhaps he is meditating on new and more distinguished shameful acts."

"Perhaps. He has not given me any word."

"But we can have confidence in him."

"Until he dies," the *Gran Maestro* said. "After that he can roast in hell and we will revere his memory."

"Giorgio," the Colonel said. "Give the *Gran Maestro* another short *Carpano*."

"If it is your order," the *Gran Maestro* said, "I can only obey."

They touched glasses.

"Jackson," the Colonel called. "You're on the town. You can sign here for chow. I don't want to see you until eleven hundred tomorrow in the lobby, unless you get into trouble. Do you have money?"

"Yes, sir," Jackson said and thought, the old son of a

bitch really *is* as crazy as they say. But he might have called me instead of shouting.

"I don't want to see you," the Colonel said.

Jackson had entered the room and stood before him at a semblance of attention.

"I'm tired of seeing you, because you worry and you don't have fun. For Christ sake have yourself some fun."

"Yes, sir."

"You understand what I said?"

"Yes, sir."

"Repeat it."

"Ronald Jackson, T5 Serial Number 100678, will present himself in the lobby of this Gritti Hotel at 1100 tomorrow morning, I don't know the date, sir, and will absent himself from the Colonel's sight and will have some fun. Or," he added, "will make every reasonable attempt to attain that objective."

"I'm sorry, Jackson," the Colonel said. "I'm a shit."

"I beg to differ with the Colonel," Jackson said.

"Thank you, Jackson," the Colonel told him. "Maybe I'm not. I hope you are correct. Now muck off. You've got a room here, or you should have, and you can sign for chow. Now try and have some fun."

"Yes, sir," said Jackson.

When he was gone, the *Gran Maestro* said to the Colonel, "What is the boy? One of those *sad* Americans?"

"Yes," the Colonel said. "And by Jesus Christ we've got a lot of them. Sad, self-righteous, over-fed and under-trained. If they are under-trained, it is my fault. But we've got some good ones, too."

"Do you think they would have done Grappa, Pasubio and the Basso Piave as we did?"

"The good ones, yes. Maybe better. But you know, in our army, they don't even shoot for self-inflicted wounds."

"Jesus," said the *Gran Maestro*. He and the Colonel both remembered the men who decided that they did not wish to die; not thinking that he who dies on Thursday does not have to die on Friday, and how one soldier would wrap another's puttee-ed leg in a sandbag so there would be no powder burns, and loose off at his friend from as far a distance as he figured he could hit the calf of the leg without hitting bone, and then fire twice over the parapet to alibi the shot. They had this knowledge shared between them and it was for this reason and for a true, good hatred of all those who profited by war that they had founded the Order.

They knew, the two of them, who loved and respected each other, how *poor* boys who did not want to die, would share the contents of a match box full of gonorrheal pus to produce the infection that would keep them from the next murderous frontal attack.

They knew about the other boys who put the big ten centime pieces under their arm-pits to produce jaundice. And they knew, too, about the richer boys who, in different cities, had paraffin injected under their knee-caps so they would not have to go to the war.

They knew how garlic could be used to produce certain effects which could absent a man from an attack, and they knew all, or nearly all, of the other tricks; for one had been a sergeant and the other a lieutenant of infantry and they had fought on the three key points, Pasubio, Grappa, and the Piave, where it all made sense.

They had fought, too, in the earlier stupid butchery on the Isonzo and the Carso. But they were both ashamed of those who had ordered that, and they never thought about it except as a shameful, stupid thing to be forgotten and the Colonel remembered it technically as something to learn from. So, now, they had founded the Order of Brusadelli; noble, military and religious, and there were only five members.

"What is the news of the Order?" the Colonel asked the *Gran Maestro.*

"We have ascended the cook at the Magnificent to the rank of Commendatore. He comported himself as a man three times on his fiftieth birthday. I accepted his statement without corroboration. He never lied ever."

"No. He never lied. But it is a topic on which you must be chary in your credibility."

"I believed him. He looked ruined."

"I can remember him when he was a tough kid and we called him the cherry buster."

"*Anch' io.*"

"Have you any concrete plans for the Order during the Winter?"

"No, Supreme Commander."

"Do you think we should give a homage to the Honorable Pacciardi?"

"As you wish."

"Let's defer it," the Colonel said. He thought a moment, and signalled for another dry Martini.

"Do you think we might organize a homage and manifestation in some historic place such as San Marco or the old church at Torcello in favor of our Great Patron, Brusadelli, the Revered One?"

"I doubt if the religious authorities would permit it at this moment."

"Then let us abandon all ideas of public manifestations for this winter, and work within our cadres, for the good of the Order."

"I think that is soundest," the *Gran Maestro* said. "We will re-group."

"And how are you, yourself?"

"Awful," the *Gran Maestro* said. "I have low blood pressure, ulcers, and I owe money."

"Are you happy?"

"All the time," the *Gran Maestro* said. "I like my work very much, and I meet extraordinary and interesting characters, also many Belgians. They are what we have instead of the locusts this year. Formerly we had the Germans. What was it Caesar said, 'And the bravest of these are the Belgians.' But not the best dressed. Do you agree?"

"I've seen them quite well costumed in Brussels," the Colonel said. "A well fed, gay capital. Win, lose, or draw. I have never seen them fight though everyone tells me that they do."

"We should have fought in Flanders in the old days."

"We were not born in the old days," the Colonel said. "So we automatically could not have fought then."

"I wish we could have fought with the Condottieri when all you had to do was out-think them and they conceded. You could think and I would convey your orders."

"We'd have to take a few towns for them to respect our thinking."

"We would sack them if they defended them," the *Gran Maestro* said. "What towns would you take?"

"Not this one," the Colonel said. "I'd take Vicenza, Bergamo and Verona. Not necessarily in that order."

"You'd have to take two more."

"I know," the Colonel said. He was a general now again, and he was happy. "I figured that I'd by-pass Brescia. It could fall of its own weight."

"And how are you, Supreme Commander?" the *Gran Maestro* said, for this taking of towns had pulled him out of his depth.

He was at home in his small house in Treviso, close to the fast flowing river under the old walls. The weeds waved in the current and the fish hung in the shelter of the weeds and rose to insects that touched the water in the dusk. He was at home, too, in all operations that did not involve more than a company, and understood them as clearly as he understood the proper serving of a small dining room; or a large dining room.

But when the Colonel became a general officer again, as he had once been, and thought in terms that were as far beyond him as calculus is distant from a man who has only the knowledge of arithmetic, then he was not at home, and their contact was strained, and he wished the Colonel would return to things they both knew together when they were a lieutenant and a sergeant.

"What would you do about Mantova?" the Colonel asked.

"I do not know, my Colonel. I do not know whom you are fighting, nor what forces they have, nor what forces are at your disposal."

"I thought you said we were Condottieri. Based on this town or on Padova."

"My Colonel," the *Gran Maestro* said, and he had diminished in no way, "I know nothing, truly, about Condottieri. Nor really how they fought then. I only said I would like to fight under you in such times."

"There aren't any such times any more," the Colonel said and the spell was broken.

What the hell, maybe there never was any spell, the Colonel thought. The hell with you, he said to himself. Cut it out and be a human being when you're half a hundred years old.

"Have another *Carpano*," he said to the *Gran Maestro*.

"My Colonel, you will allow me to refuse because of the ulcers?"

"Yes. Yes. Of course. Boy, what's your name, Giorgio? Another dry Martini. *Secco, molto secco e doppio*."

Breaking spells, he thought. It is not my trade. My trade is killing armed men. A spell should be armed if I'm to

63

break it. But we have killed many things which were not armed. All right, spell breaker, retract.

"*Gran Maestro,*" he said. "You are still *Gran Maestro* and fornicate the Condottieri."

"They were fornicated many years ago, Supreme Commander."

"Exactly," the Colonel said.

But the spell was broken.

"I'll see you at dinner," the Colonel said. "What is there?"

"We will have anything you wish, and what we do not have I will send out for."

"Do you have any fresh asparagus?"

"You know we cannot have it in these months. It comes in April and from Bassano."

"Then I'll just urinate the usual odor," the Colonel said. "You think of something and I'll eat it."

"How many will you be?" the Maitre d'Hotel asked.

"We'll be two," the Colonel said. "What time do you close the *bistro?*"

"We will serve dinner as late as you wish to eat, my Colonel."

"I'll try to be in at a sound hour," the Colonel said. "Good-bye, *Gran Maestro,*" he said and smiled, and gave the *Gran Maestro* his crooked hand.

"Good-bye, Supreme Commander," said the *Gran Maestro* and the spell was existent again and almost complete.

But it was not quite complete and the Colonel knew it

and he thought: why am I always a bastard and why can I not suspend this trade of arms, and be a kind and good man as I would have wished to be.

I try always to be just, but I am brusque and I am brutal, and it is not that I have erected the defense against brown-nosing my superiors and brown-nosing the world. I should be a better man with less wild boar blood in the small time which remains. We will try it out tonight, he thought. With whom, he thought, and where, and God help me not to be bad.

"Giorgio," he said to the barman, who had a face as white as a leper, but with no bulges, and without the silver shine.

Giorgio did not really like the Colonel very much, or perhaps he was simply from Piemonte, and cared for no one truly; which was understandable in cold people from a border province. Borderers are not trusters, and the Colonel knew about this, and expected nothing from anyone that they did not have to give.

"Giorgio," he said to the pale-faced barman. "Write these down for me, please."

He went out, walking as he had always walked, with a slightly exaggerated confidence, even when it was not needed, and, in his always renewed plan of being kind, decent and good, he greeted the concierge, who was a friend, the assistant manager, who spoke Swahili and had been a prisoner of war in Kenya, and was a most amiable man, young, full of juice, handsome, perhaps not yet a member of the Order, and experienced.

"And the *cavaliere ufficiale* who manages this place?" he asked. "My friend?"

"He is not here," the assistant manager said. "For the moment, naturally," he added.

"Give him my compliments," the Colonel said. "And have somebody show me to my room."

"It is the usual room. You still wish it?"

"Yes. Have you taken care of the Sergeant?"

"He is well taken care of."

"Good," said the Colonel.

The Colonel proceeded to his room accompanied by the boy who carried his bag.

"This way, my Colonel," the boy said, when the elevator halted with slight hydraulic inaccuracy at the top floor.

"Can't you run an elevator properly?" the Colonel asked.

"No, my Colonel," the boy said. "The current is not stable."

CHAPTER VIII

THE Colonel said nothing and preceded the boy down the corridor. It was large, wide and high ceilinged, and there was a long and distinguished interval between the doors of the rooms on the side of the Grand Canal. Naturally, since it had been a palace, there were no rooms without excellent views, except those which had been made for the servants.

The Colonel found the walk long, although it was a very short one, and when the waiter who served the room appeared, short, dark and with his glass eye in the left eye socket gleaming, unable to smile his full, true smile as he worked the big key in the lock, the Colonel wished that the door would open more rapidly.

"Open it up," he said.

"I will, my Colonel," the waiter said. "But you know these locks."

Yes, the Colonel thought. I know them, but I wish that he would get it open.

"How are your family?" he said to the waiter, who had swung the door wide so that the Colonel, now entered, was within the room with the high, dark but well-mirrored armoire, the two good beds, the great chandelier and the view, through the still closed windows, onto the wind beaten water of the Grand Canal.

The Canal was grey as steel now in the quick, failing, winter light and the Colonel said, "Arnaldo, open the windows."

"There is much wind, my Colonel, and the room is badly heated due to the lack of electric power."

"Due to the lack of rainfall," the Colonel said. "Open the windows. All of them."

"As you wish, my Colonel."

The waiter opened the windows and the north wind came into the room.

"Please call the desk and ask them to ring this number." The waiter made the call while the Colonel was in the bathroom.

"The Contessa is not at home, my Colonel," he said. "They believe you might find her at Harry's."

"You find everything on earth at Harry's."

"Yes, my Colonel. Except, possibly, happiness."

"I'll damn well find happiness, too," the Colonel assured him. "Happiness, as you know, is a movable feast."

"I am aware of that," the waiter said. "I have brought

68

Campari bitters and a bottle of Gordon Gin. May I make you a Campari with gin and soda?"

"You're a good boy," the Colonel said. "Where did you bring them from. The bar?"

"No. I bought them while you were away so that you would not have to spend money at the bar. The bar is very costly."

"I agree," the Colonel agreed. "But you should not use your own money on such a project."

"I took a chance. We have both taken many. The gin was 3200 lire and is legitimate. The Campari was 800."

"You're a very good boy," the Colonel told him. "How were the ducks?"

"My wife still speaks of them. We had never had wild ducks, since they are of such expense, and outside of our way of life. But one of our neighbors told her how to prepare them and these same neighbors ate them with us. I never knew that anything could be so wonderful to eat. When your teeth close on the small slice of meat it is an almost unbelievable delight."

"I think so, too. There is nothing lovelier to eat than those fat iron-curtain ducks. You know their fly-way is through the great grain fields of the Danube. This is a splinter flight we have here, but they always come the same way since before there were shot-guns."

"I know nothing about shooting for sport," the waiter said. "We were too poor."

"But many people without money shoot in the Veneto."

"Yes. Of course. One hears them shoot all night. But we

were poorer than that. We were poorer than you can know, my Colonel."

"I think I can know."

"Perhaps," the waiter said. "My wife also saved all the feathers and she asked me to thank you."

"If we have any luck day after tomorrow, we'll get plenty. The big ducks with the green heads. Tell your wife, with luck, there will be good eating ducks, fat as pigs with what they have eaten from the Russians, and with beautiful feathers."

"How do you feel about the Russians, if it is not indiscreet to ask, my Colonel?"

"They are our potential enemy. So, as a soldier, I am prepared to fight them. But I like them very much and I have never known finer people nor people more as we are."

"I have never had the good fortune to know them."

"You will, boy. You will. Unless the Honorable Pacciardi stops them on the line of the Piave, which is a river which no longer contains water. It has been syphoned off for hydro-electric projects. Perhaps the Honorable Pacciardi will fight there. But I do not think he will fight for long."

"I do not know the Honorable Pacciardi."

"I know him," said the Colonel.

"Now ask them to ring Harry's and see if the Contessa is there. If not, have them ring the house again."

The Colonel took the drink Arnaldo, the glass-eyed waiter, made him. He did not want it, and he knew that it was bad for him.

But he took it with his old wild-boar truculence, as he had taken everything all of his life, and he moved, still cat-like when he moved, although it was an old cat now, over to the open window and looked out on the great Canal which was now becoming as grey as though Degas had painted it on one of his greyest days.

"Thanks very much for the drink," the Colonel said, and Arnaldo, who was talking into the telephone, nodded and smiled his glass-eyed smile.

I wish he did not have to have that glass eye, the Colonel thought. He only loved people, he thought, who had fought or been mutilated.

Other people were fine and you liked them and were good friends; but you only felt true tenderness and love for those who had been there and had received the castigation that everyone receives who goes there long enough.

So I'm a sucker for crips, he thought, drinking the unwanted drink. And any son of a bitch who has been hit solidly, as every man will be if he stays, then I love him.

Yes, his other, good, side said. You love them.

I'd rather not love anyone, the Colonel thought. I'd rather have fun.

And fun, his good side said to him, you have no fun when you do not love.

All right. I love more than any son of the great bitch alive, the Colonel said, but not aloud.

Aloud, he said, "Where are you getting on that call, Arnaldo?"

"Cipriani has not come in," the waiter said. "They are

expecting him at any moment and I am keeping the line open in case he arrives."

"A costly procedure," the Colonel said. "Get me a reading on who's there so we don't waste time. I want to know exactly who is there."

Arnaldo spoke guardedly into the mouthpiece of the telephone.

He covered the mouth of the phone with his hand and said, "I am talking to Ettore. He says the Barone Alvarito is not there. The Count Andrea is there and he is rather drunk, Ettore says, but not too drunk for you to have fun together. The group of ladies that comes in each afternoon are there and there is a Greek Princess, that you know, and several people that you do not know. Riff-raff from the American Consulate who have stayed on since noon."

"Tell him to call back when the riff-raff goes and I'll come over."

Arnaldo spoke into the phone, then turned to the Colonel who was looking out of the window at the Dome of the Dogana, "Ettore says he will try to move them, but he is afraid Cipriani will not like it."

"Tell him not to move them. They don't have to work this afternoon and there is no reason why they should not get drunk like any other man. I just don't want to see them."

"Ettore says he will call back. He told me to tell you he thinks the position will fall of its own weight."

"Thank him for calling," the Colonel said.

He watched a gondola working up the Canal against

the wind and thought, not with Americans drinking. I know they are bored. In this town, too. They are bored in this town. I know the place is cold and their wages are inadequate and what fuel costs. I admire their wives, for the valiant efforts they make to transport Keokuk to Venice, and their children already speak Italian like little Venetians. But no snapshots today, Jack. Today we are giving the snapshots, the barroom confidences, the unwanted comradely drinks and the tedious woes of the Consular services a miss.

"No second, third or fourth vice-consuls today, Arnaldo."

"There are some very pleasant people from the Consulate."

"Yeah," the Colonel said. "They had a hell of a nice consul here in 1918. Everybody liked him. I'll try to remember his name."

"You go back a long way back, my Colonel."

"I go back so damn far back that it isn't funny."

"Do you remember everything from the old days?"

"Everything," the Colonel said. "Carroll was the man's name."

"I have heard of him."

"You weren't born then."

"Do you think it is necessary to have been born at the time to know about things that have happened in this town, my Colonel?"

"You're perfectly correct. Tell me, does everybody always know about everything that happens in this town?"

"Not everybody. But nearly everybody," the waiter said. "After all, sheets are sheets and some one has to change them, and some one has to wash them. Naturally I do not refer to the sheets in a hotel such as this."

"I've had some damn good times in my life without sheets."

"Naturally. But the gondoliers, while they are the most cooperative and, for me, the finest people that we have, speak among themselves."

"Naturally."

"Then the clergy. While they would never violate the secrecy of the confessional, talk among themselves."

"It is to be expected."

"Their housekeepers talk among themselves."

"It is their right."

"Then the waiters," Arnaldo said. "People talk at a table as though the waiter were stone-deaf. The waiter, according to his ethics, makes no attempt to ever overhear a conversation. But sometimes he cannot escape from hearing. Naturally, we have our own conversations among ourselves. Never in this hotel of course. I could go on."

"I believe I get the point."

"Not to mention the coiffeurs and the hair-dressers."

"And what's the news from the Rialto now?"

"You will get it all at Harry's except the part you figure in."

"Do I figure?"

"Everyone knows everything."

"Well, it's a damn pleasant story."

74

"Some people don't understand the Torcello part."

"I'm damned if I do sometimes myself."

"How old are you, my Colonel, if it is not too indiscreet to ask?"

"Fifty plus one. Why didn't you find out from the concierge? I fill out a slip there for the Questura."

"I wanted to hear it from you yourself and to congratulate you."

"I don't know what you are talking about."

"Let me congratulate you anyway."

"I can't accept it."

"You are very well liked in this city."

"Thank you. That is a very great compliment."

Just then the telephone buzzed.

"I'll take it," the Colonel said and heard Ettore's voice say, "Who speaks?"

"Colonel Cantwell."

"The position has fallen, my Colonel."

"Which way did they go?"

"Toward the Piazza."

"Good. I will be there at once."

"Do you want a table?"

"In the corner," said the Colonel and hung up.

"I am off for Harry's."

"Good hunting."

"I hunt ducks day after tomorrow before first light in a *botte* in the marshes."

"It will be cold, too."

"I dare say," the Colonel said and put on his trench coat

and looked at his face in the glass of the long mirror as he put on his cap.

"An ugly face," he said to the glass. "Did you ever see a more ugly face?"

"Yes," said Arnaldo. "Mine. Every morning when I shave."

"We both ought to shave in the dark," the Colonel told him, and went out the door.

CHAPTER IX

AS Colonel Cantwell stepped out of the door of the Gritti Palace Hotel he came out into the last sunlight of that day. There was still sunlight on the opposite side of the Square but the gondoliers preferred to be sheltered from the cold wind by lounging in the lee of the Gritti, than to use the last remaining heat of the sun on the wind-swept side of the Square.

After noting this, the Colonel turned to the right and walked along the Square to the paved street which turned off on the right. As he turned, he stopped for a moment and looked at the church of Santa Maria del Giglio.

What a fine, compact and, yet, ready to be air-borne building, he thought. I never realized a small church could look like a P47. Must find out when it was built, and who built it. Damn, I wish I might walk around this town all my life. All my life, he thought. What a gag that is. A gag to gag on. A throttle to throttle you with. Come on, boy, he said to himself. No horse named Morbid ever won a race.

Besides, he thought, as he looked in the windows of the various shops he passed, the charcuterie with the Parmesan cheeses and the hams from San Daniele, and the sausages alla cacciatora, and the bottles of good Scotch whisky and real Gordon's gin, the cutlery store, an antique dealer's with some good pieces and some old maps and prints, a second-rate restaurant disguised expensively as one of the first class, and then came to the first bridge crossing a feeder canal with steps to be climbed, I don't feel so badly. There is only the buzzing. I remember when that started and I thought perhaps it was seven year locusts in the trees and I did not like to ask young Lowry but I did. And he answered, No, General, I don't hear any crickets or seven year locusts. The night is perfectly quiet except for the usual noises.

Then, as he climbed, he felt the twinges, and coming down the other side, he saw two lovely looking girls. They were beautiful and hatless and poorly but chicly dressed, and they were talking very fast to each other and the wind was blowing their hair as they climbed with their long, easy striding Venetian legs and the Colonel said to himself, I'd better quit window gazing along this street and make that next bridge, and two squares afterwards you turn due right and keep along it till you are in Harry's.

He did just that, twinging on the bridge, but walking with his same old stride and only seeing, quickly, the people

78

that he passed. There's a lot of oxygen in this air, he thought, as he faced into the wind and breathed deeply.

Then he was pulling open the door of Harry's bar and was inside and he had made it again, and was at home.

At the bar a tall, very tall, man, with a ravaged face of great breeding, merry blue eyes, and the long, loose-coupled body of a buffalo wolf, said, "My ancient and depraved Colonel."

"My wicked Andrea."

They embraced and the Colonel felt the rough texture of Andrea's handsome tweed coat that must have been entering, at least, its twentieth year.

"You look well, Andrea," the Colonel said.

It was a lie and they both knew it.

"I am," said Andrea, returning the lie. "I must say I never felt better. You look extraordinarily well, yourself."

"Thank you, Andrea. Us healthy bastards shall inherit the earth."

"Very good idea. I must say I wouldn't mind inheriting something these days."

"You have no kick. You'll inherit well over six feet four of it."

"Six feet six," said Andrea. "You wicked old man. Are you still slaving away at *la vie militaire?*"

"I don't slave too hard at it," the Colonel said. "I'm down to shoot at San Relajo."

"I know. But don't make jokes in Spanish at this hour. Alvarito was looking for you. He said to tell you he'd be back."

"Good. Is your lovely wife and are the children well?"

"Absolutely, and they asked me to remember them to you if I saw you. They're down in Rome. There comes your girl. Or one of your girls." He was so tall he could see into the now almost dark street, but this was a girl you could recognize if it was much darker than it was at this hour.

"Ask her to have a drink with us here before you carry her off to that corner table. Isn't she a lovely girl?"

"She is."

Then she came into the room, shining in her youth and tall striding beauty, and the carelessness the wind had made of her hair. She had pale, almost olive colored skin, a profile that could break your, or any one else's heart, and her dark hair, of an alive texture, hung down over her shoulders.

"Hello, my great beauty," the Colonel said.

"Oh, oh, hello," she said. "I thought I would miss you. I am so sorry to be late."

Her voice was low and delicate and she spoke English with caution.

"*Ciao*, Andrea," she said. "How is Emily and are the children?"

"Probably just the same as when I answered that same question for you at noon."

"I am so sorry," she said and blushed. "I am so excited and I always say the wrong things. What should I say? Have you had a good time here all afternoon?"

"Yes," said Andrea. "With my old friend and severest critic."

"Who is that?"

"Scotch whisky and water."

"I suppose if he must tease me he must," she said to the Colonel. "But you won't tease me, will you?"

"Take him over to that corner table and talk to him. I'm tired of you both."

"I'm not tired of you," the Colonel told him. "But I think it is a good idea. Should we have a drink sitting down, Renata?"

"I'd love to if Andrea isn't angry."

"I'm never angry."

"Would you have a drink with us, Andrea?"

"No," said Andrea. "Get along to your table. I'm sick of seeing it unoccupied."

"Good-bye, Caro. Thanks for the drink we didn't have."

"*Ciao*, Ricardo," Andrea said and that was all.

He turned his fine, long, tall back on them and looked into the mirror that is placed behind bars so a man can tell when he is drinking too much, and decided that he did not like what he saw there. "Ettore," he said. "Please put this nonsense on my bill."

He walked out after waiting carefully for his coat, swinging into it, and tipping the man who brought it exactly what he should be tipped plus twenty per cent.

At the corner table, Renata said, "Do you think we hurt his feelings?"

"No. He loves you and he likes me."

"Andrea is so nice. And you're so nice."

"Waiter," the Colonel called; then asked, "Do you want a dry Martini, too?"

"Yes," she said. "I'd love one."

"Two very dry Martinis," the Colonel said. "Montgomerys. Fifteen to one."

The waiter, who had been in the desert, smiled and was gone, and the Colonel turned to Renata.

"You're nice," he said. "You're also very beautiful and lovely and I love you."

"You always say that and I don't know what it means but I like to hear it."

"How old are you now?"

"Nearly nineteen. Why?"

"And you don't know what it means?"

"No. Why should I? Americans always say it to you before they go away. It seems to be necessary to them. But I love you very much, too, whatever that is."

"Let's have a fine time," the Colonel said. "Let's not think about anything at all."

"I would like that. I cannot think very well this time of day at any rate."

"Here are the drinks," the Colonel said. "Remember not to say, chin-chin."

"I remember that from before. I never say chin-chin, nor here's to you, nor bottom's up."

"We just raise the glass to each other and, if you wish, we can touch the edges."

"I wish," she said.

The Martinis were icy cold and true Montgomerys, and,

after touching the edges, they felt them glow happily all through their upper bodies.

"And what have you been doing?" the Colonel asked.

"Nothing. I still wait to go away to school."

"Where now?"

"God knows. Wherever I go to learn English."

"Turn your head and raise your chin once for me."

"You're not making fun?"

"No. I'm not making fun."

She turned her head and raised her chin, without vanity, nor coquetry, and the Colonel felt his heart turn over inside him, as though some sleeping animal had rolled over in its burrow and frightened, deliciously, the other animal sleeping close beside.

"Oh you," he said. "Would you ever like to run for Queen of Heaven?"

"That would be sacrilegious."

"Yes," he said. "I suppose it would and I withdraw the suggestion."

"Richard," she said. "No I can't say it."

"Say it."

"No."

The Colonel thought, I order you to say it. And she said, "Please never look at me like that."

"I'm sorry," the Colonel said. "I had just slipped into my trade unconsciously."

"And if we were such a thing as married would you practice your trade in the home?"

"No. I swear it. I never have. Not in my heart."

"With no one?"

"With no one of your sex."

"I don't like that word your sex. It sounds as though you were practicing your trade."

"I throw my trade out of that God-damn window into the Grand Canal."

"There," she said. "You see how quickly you practice it?"

"All right," he said. "I love you and my trade can gently leave."

"Let me feel your hand," she said. "It's all right. You can put it on the table."

"Thank you," the Colonel said.

"Please don't," she said. "I wanted to feel it because all last week, every night, or I think nearly every night, I dreamed about it, and it was a strange mixed-up dream and I dreamed it was the hand of Our Lord."

"That's bad. You oughtn't to do that."

"I know it. That's just what I dreamed."

"You aren't on the junk, are you?"

"I don't know what you mean, and please don't make fun when I tell you something true. I dreamed just as I say."

"What did the hand do?"

"Nothing. Or maybe that is not true. Mostly it was just a hand."

"Like this one?" The Colonel asked, looking at the misshapen hand with distaste, and remembering the two times that had made it that way.

"Not like. It *was* that one. May I touch it carefully with my fingers if it does not hurt?"

"It does not hurt. Where it hurts is in the head, the legs and the feet. I don't believe there's any sensation in that hand."

"You're wrong," she said. "Richard. There is very much sensation in that hand."

"I don't like to look at it much. You don't think we could skip it."

"Of course. But you don't have to dream about it."

"No. I have other dreams."

"Yes. I can imagine. But I dream lately about this hand. Now that I have touched it carefully, we can talk about funny things if you like. What is there funny we should talk about?"

"Let's look at the people and discuss them."

"That's lovely," she said. "And we won't do it with malice. Only with our best wit. Yours and mine."

"Good," the Colonel said. "Waiter, *Ancora due Martini.*"

He did not like to call for Montgomerys in a tone that could be overheard because there were two obvious Britishers at the next table.

The male might have been wounded, the Colonel thought, although, from his looks, it seems unlikely. But God help me to avoid brutality. And look at Renata's eyes, he thought. They are probably the most beautiful of all the beautiful things she has, with the longest honest lashes I have ever seen and she never uses them for anything except to look at you honestly and straight. What a damn wonderful girl and what am I doing here anyway? It is wicked. She is your last and true and only love, he thought, and that's not evil. It is only unfortunate. No, he thought, it is damned fortunate and you are very fortunate.

They sat at a small table in the corner of the room and on their right there were four women at a larger table. One of the women was in mourning; a mourning so theatrical that it reminded the Colonel of the Lady Diana Manners playing the nun in Max Reinhardt's, "The Miracle." This woman had an attractive, plump, naturally gay face and her mourning was incongruous.

At the table there was another woman who had hair three times as white as hair can be, the Colonel thought. She, also, had a pleasant face. There were two other women whose faces meant nothing to the Colonel.

"Are they lesbians?" he asked the girl.

"I do not know," she said. "They are all very nice people."

"I should say they are lesbians. But maybe they are just good friends. Maybe they are both. It means nothing to me and it was not a criticism."

"You are nice when you are gentle."

"Do you suppose the word gentleman derives from a man who is gentle?"

"I do not know," the girl said, and she ran her fingers very lightly over the scarred hand. "But I love you when you are gentle."

"I'll try very hard to be gentle," the Colonel said. "Who do you suppose that son of a bitch is at the table beyond them?"

"You don't stay gentle very long," the girl said. "Let us ask Ettore."

They looked at the man at the third table. He had a strange face like an over-enlarged, disappointed weasel or ferret. It looked as pock-marked and as blemished as the mountains of the moon seen through a cheap telescope and, the Colonel thought, it looked like Goebbels' face, if Herr Goebbels had ever been in a plane that burned, and not been able to bail out before the fire reached him.

Above this face, which was ceaselessly peering, as though the answer might be found by enough well directed glances and by queries, there was black hair that seemed to have no connection with the human race. The man looked as though he had been scalped and then the hair replaced. Very interesting, the Colonel thought. Can he be a compatriot? Yes, he must.

A little spit ran out of the corner of his mouth as he spoke, peeringly, with the elderly, wholesome looking woman who was with him. She looks like anybody's mother in an illustration in "The Ladies' Home Journal," the Colonel thought. "The Ladies' Home Journal" was one of the magazines received regularly at the Officer's Club in Trieste and the Colonel looked through it when it came. It is a wonderful magazine, he thought, because it combines sexology and beautiful foods. It makes me hungry both ways.

But who do you suppose that character is? He looks like a caricature of an American who has been run one half way through a meat chopper and then been boiled, slightly, in oil. I'm not being so gentle, he thought.

Ettore, with his emaciated face, and his love of joking and fundamental and abiding disrespect, came over and the Colonel said, "Who is that spiritual character?"

Ettore shook his head.

The man was short and dark with glossy black hair that did not seem to go with his strange face. He looked, the Colonel thought, as though he had forgotten to change his wig as he grew older. Has a wonderful face though, the Colonel thought. Looks like some of the hills around Verdun. I don't suppose he could be Goebbels and he picked up that face in the last days when they were all playing at Götterdämmerung. *Komm' Süsser Tod*, he thought. Well they sure bought themselves a nice big piece of Süsser Tod at the end.

"You don't want a nice Süsser Tod sandwich do you Miss Renata?"

"I don't think so," the girl said· "Though I love Bach and I am sure Cipriani could make one."

"I was not talking against Bach," the Colonel said.

"I know it."

"Hell," the Colonel said. "Bach was practically a co-belligerent. As you were," he added.

"I don't think we have to talk against me."

"Daughter," the Colonel said. "When will you learn that I might joke against you because I love you?"

88

"Now," she said. "I've learned it. But you know it's fun not to joke too rough."

"Good. I've learned it."

"How often do you think of me during the week?"

"All of the time."

"No. Tell me truly."

"All of the time. Truly."

"Do you think it is this bad for everyone?"

"I wouldn't know," the Colonel said. "That's one of the things I would not know."

"I hope it's not this bad for everyone. I had no idea it could be this bad."

"Well you know now."

"Yes," the girl said. "I know now. I know now and for keeps and for always. Is that the correct way to say it?"

"I know now is enough," the Colonel said. "Ettore, that character with the inspiring face and the nice looking woman with him doesn't live at the Gritti does he?"

"No," Ettore said. "He lives next door but he goes to the Gritti sometimes to eat."

"Good," the Colonel said. "It will be wonderful to see him if I should ever be down hearted. Who is the woman with him? His wife? His mother? His daughter?

"There you have me," Ettore said. "We haven't kept track of him in Venice. He has aroused neither love, hate, dislike, fear nor suspicion. Do you really want to know anything about him? I could ask Cipriani."

"Let us skip him," the girl said. "Is that how you say it?"

"Let's skip him," the Colonel said.

"When we have so little time, Richard. He is rather a waste of time."

"I was looking at him as at a drawing by Goya. Faces are pictures too."

"Look at mine and I will look at yours. Please skip the man. He didn't come here to do anyone any harm."

"Let me look at your face and you not look at mine."

"No," she said. "That's not fair. I have to remember yours all week."

"And what do I do?" the Colonel asked her.

Ettore came over, unable to avoid conspiracy and, having gathered his intelligence rapidly and as a Venetian should, said,

"My colleague who works at his hotel, says that he drinks three or four highballs, and then writes vastly and fluently far into the night."

"I dare say that makes marvelous reading."

"I dare say," Ettore said. "But it was hardly the method of Dante."

"Dante was another *vieux con*," the Colonel said. "I mean as a man. Not as a writer."

"I agree," Ettore said. "I think you will find no one, outside of Firenze, who has studied his life who would not agree."

"Eff Florence," the Colonel said.

"A difficult maneuver," Ettore said. "Many have attempted it but very few have succeeded. Why do you dislike it, my Colonel?"

"Too complicated to explain. But it was the depot," he said *deposito*, "of my old regiment when I was a boy."

"That I can understand. I have my own reasons for disliking it too. You know a good town?"

"Yes," said the Colonel. "This one. A part of Milano; and Bologna. And Bergamo."

"Cipriani has a large store of vodka in case the Russians should come," Ettore said, loving to joke rough.

"They'll bring their own vodka, duty free."

"Still I believe Cipriani is prepared for them."

"Then he is the only man who is," the Colonel said. "Tell him not to take any checks from junior officers on the Bank of Odessa, and thank you for the data on my compatriot. I won't take more of your time."

Ettore left and the girl turned toward him, and looked in his old steel eyes and put both her hands on his bad one and said, "You were quite gentle."

"And you are most beautiful and I love you."

"It's nice to hear it anyway."

"What are we going to do about dinner?"

"I will have to call my home and find out if I can come out."

"Why do you look sad now?"

"Do I?"

"Yes."

"I am not, really. I am as happy as I ever am. Truly. Please believe me, Richard. But how would you like to be a girl nineteen years old in love with a man over fifty years old that you knew was going to die?"

"You put it a little bluntly," the Colonel said. "But you are very beautiful when you say it."

"I never cry," the girl said. "Never. I made a rule not to. But I would cry now."

"Don't cry," the Colonel said. "I'm gentle now and the hell with the rest of it."

"Say once again that you love me."

"I love you and I love you and I love you."

"Will you do your best not to die?"

"Yes."

"What did the doctor say?"

"So-so."

"Not worse?"

"No," he lied.

"Then let us have another Martini," the girl said. "You know I never drank a Martini until we met."

"I know. But you drink them awfully well."

"Shouldn't you take the medicine?"

"Yes," the Colonel said. "I should take the medicine."

"May I give it to you?"

"Yes," the Colonel said. "You may give it to me."

They continued to sit at the table in the corner and some people went out, and others came in. The Colonel felt a little dizzy from the medicine and he let it ride. That's the way it always is, he thought. To hell with it.

He saw the girl watching him and he smiled at her. It was an old smile that he had been using for fifty years, ever since he first smiled, and it was still as sound as your grandfather's Purdey shot-gun. I guess my older brother has that, he thought. Well, he could always shoot better than I could and he deserves it.

"Listen, daughter," he said. "Don't be sorry for me."

"I'm not. Not at all. I just love you."

"It isn't much of a trade is it?" He said *oficio* instead of trade, because they spoke Spanish together too, when they left French, and when they did not wish to speak English before other people. Spanish is a rough language, the Colonel thought, rougher than a corncob sometimes. But you can say what you mean in it and make it stick.

"*Es un oficio bastante malo,*" he repeated, "loving me."

"Yes. But it is the only one I have."

"Don't you write any more poetry?"

"It was young girl poetry. Like young girl painting. Everyone is talented at a certain age."

At what age do you become old in this country, the Colonel thought. No one is ever old in Venice, but they grow up very fast. I grew up very rapidly in the Veneto myself, and I was never as old as I was at twenty-one.

"How is your mother?" he asked, lovingly.

"She is very well. She does not receive and she sees almost no one because of her sorrow."

"Do you think she would mind if we had a baby?"

"I don't know. She is very intelligent, you know. But I would have to marry someone, I suppose. I don't really want to."

"We could be married."

"No," she said. "I thought it over, and I thought we should not. It is just a decision as the one about crying."

93

"Maybe you make wrong decisions. Christ knows I've made a few and too many men are dead from when I was wrong."

"I think, perhaps, you exaggerate. I don't believe you made many wrong decisions."

"Not many," the Colonel said. "But enough. Three is plenty in my trade, and I made all three."

"I'd like to know about them."

"They'd bore you," the Colonel told her. "They beat the hell out of me to remember them. So what would they do to some outsider?"

"Am I an outsider?"

"No. You're my true love. My last and only and true love."

"Did you make them early or late? The decisions."

"I made them early. In the middle. And late."

"Wouldn't you tell me about them? I would like to have a share in your sad trade."

"The hell with them," the Colonel said. "They were made and they've all been paid for. Only you can't pay for that."

"Can you tell me about that and why?"

"No," the Colonel said. And that was the end of that.

"Then let's have fun."

"Let's," the Colonel said. "With our one and only life."

"Maybe there are others. Other lives."

"I don't think so," the Colonel said. "Turn your head sideways, beauty."

"Like this?"

"Like that," the Colonel said. "Exactly like that."

So, the Colonel thought, here we come into the last round and I do not know even the number of the round. I have loved but three women and have lost them thrice.

You lose them the same way you lose a battalion; by errors of judgment; orders that are impossible to fulfill, and through impossible conditions. Also through brutality.

I have lost three battalions in my life and three women and now I have a fourth, and loveliest, and where the hell does it end?

You tell me, General, and, incidentally, while we are discussing the matter, and it is a frank discussion of the situation and in no sense a Council of War, as you have so often pointed out to me General: GENERAL WHERE IS YOUR CAVALRY?

I have thought so, he said to himself. The Commanding Officer does not know where his cavalry is, and his cavalry are not completely accurate as to their situation, nor their mission, and they will, some of them, *enough*, muck off as cavalry have always mucked off in all the wars since they, the Cavalry, had the big horses.

"Beauty," he said, "*Ma très chère et bien aimée.* I am very dull and I am sorry."

"You are never dull, to me, and I love you and I only wish we could be cheerful tonight."

"We damn well will be," said the Colonel. "Do you know anything particular we should be cheerful about?"

"We might be cheerful about us, and about the town. You've often been very cheerful."

"Yes," the Colonel agreed. "I have been."

"Don't you think we could do it once more?"

"Sure. Of course. Why not?"

"Do you see the boy with the wave in his hair, that is natural, and he only pushes it a little, skillfully, to be more handsome?"

"I see him," the Colonel said.

"He is a very good painter, but he has false teeth in front because he was a little bit *pédéraste* once and other *pédérastes* attacked him one night on the Lido when there was a full moon."

"How old are you?"

"I will be nineteen."

"How do you know this?"

"I know it from the Gondoliere. This boy is a very good painter, for now. There aren't any really good painters now. But with false teeth, now, in his twenty-fifth year, what a thing."

"I love you very truly," the Colonel said.

"I love you very truly, too. Whatever that means in American. I also love you in Italian, against all my judgment and all of my wishes."

"We shouldn't wish for too God-damn much," the Colonel said. "Because we are always liable to get it."

"I agree," she said. "But I would like to get what I wish for now."

Neither of them said anything and then the girl said, "That boy, he is a man now, of course, and goes with very many women to hide what he is, painted my portrait once. You can have it if you like."

"Thank you," the Colonel said. "I would love it."

"It is very romantic. My hair is twice as long as it has ever been and I look as though I were rising from the sea without the head wet. Actually, you rise from the sea with the hair very flat and coming to points at the end. It is almost the look of a very nearly dead rat. But Daddy paid him adequately for the portrait, and, while it is not truly me, it is the way you like to think of me."

"I think of you when you come from the sea too."

"Of course. Very ugly. But you might like to have this portrait for a souvenir."

"Your lovely mother would not mind?"

"Mummy would not mind. She would be glad to be rid of it, I think. We have better pictures in the house."

"I love you and your mother both very much."

"I must tell her," the girl said.

"Do you think that pock-marked jerk is really a writer?"

"Yes. If Ettore says so. He loves to joke but he does not lie. Richard, what is a jerk? Tell me truly."

"It is a little rough to state. But I think it means a man who has never worked at his trade (*oficio*) truly, and is presumptuous in some annoying way."

"I must learn to use the term properly."

"Don't use it," the Colonel said.

Then the Colonel asked, "When do I get the portrait?"

"Tonight if you wish it. I'll have someone wrap it and send it from the house. Where will you hang it?"

"In my quarters."

"And no one will come in and make remarks and speak badly of me?"

"No. They damn well will not. Also I'll tell them it is a portrait of my daughter."

"Did you ever have a daughter?"

"No. I always wanted one."

"I can be your daughter as well as everything else."

"That would be incest."

"I don't think that would be so terrible in a city as old as this and that has seen what this city has seen."

"Listen, Daughter."

"Good," she said. "That was fine. I liked it."

"All right," the Colonel said and his voice was thickened a little. "I liked it, too."

"Do you see now why I love you when I know better than to do it?"

"Look, Daughter. Where should we dine?"

"Wherever you like."

"Would you eat at the Gritti?"

"Of course."

"Then call the house and ask for permission."

"No. I decided not to ask permission but to send word where I was dining. So they would not worry."

"But do you really prefer the Gritti?"

"I do. Because it is a lovely restaurant and it is where you live and anyone can look at us that wants to."

"When did you get like that?"

"I have always been like that. I have never cared what anyone thought, ever. Nor have I ever done anything that I was ashamed of except tell lies when I was a little girl and be unkind to people."

"I wish we could be married and have five sons," the Colonel said.

"So do I," the girl said. "And send them to the five corners of the world."

"Are there five corners to the world?"

"I don't know," she said. "It sounded as though there were when I said it. And now we are having fun again, aren't we?"

"Yes, Daughter," the Colonel said.

"Say it again. Just as you said it."

"Yes, Daughter."

"Oh," she said. "People must be very complicated. Please may I take your hand?"

"It's so damned ugly and I dislike looking at it."

"You don't know about your hand."

"That's a matter of opinion," he said. "I'd say you were wrong, Daughter."

"Maybe I am wrong. But we're having fun again and whatever the bad thing was is gone now."

"It's gone the way the mist is burned off the hollows in broken ground when the sun comes out," the Colonel said. "And you're the sun."

"I want to be the moon, too."

"You are," the Colonel told her. "Also any particular planet that you wish to be and I will give you an accurate location of the planet. Christ, Daughter, you can be a God-damn constellation if you like. Only that's an airplane."

"I'll be the moon. She has many troubles too."

"Yes. Her sorrows come regularly. But she always fills before she wanes."

"She looks so sad to me sometimes across the Canal that I cannot stand it."

"She's been around a long time," the Colonel said.

"Do you think we should have one more Montgomery?" the girl asked and the Colonel noticed that the British were gone.

He had been noticing nothing but her lovely face. I'll get killed sometime that way, he thought. On the other hand it is a form of concentration, I suppose. But it is damned careless.

"Yes," he said. "Why not?"

"They make me feel very good," the girl said.

"They have a certain effect on me, too, the way Cipriani makes them."

"Cipriani is very intelligent."

"He's more than that. He's able."

"Some day he'll own all Venice."

"Not quite all," the Colonel disagreed. "He'll never own you."

"No," she said. "Nor will anyone else unless you want me."

"I want you Daughter. But I don't want to own you."

"I know it," the girl said. "And that's one more reason why I love you."

"Let's get Ettore and have him call up your house. You can tell them about the portrait."

"You are quite correct. If you want the portrait tonight,

I must speak to the butler to have it wrapped and sent. I will also ask to speak to Mummy and tell her where we are dining and, if you like, I will ask her permission."

"No," the Colonel said. "Ettore, two Montgomerys, super Montgomerys, with garlic olives, not the big ones, and please call the home of this lady and let her know when you have completed the communication. And all of this as rapidly as possible."

"Yes, my Colonel."

"Now, Daughter, let us resume the having of the fun."

"It was resumed when you spoke," she said.

CHAPTER X

THEY were walking, now, along the right side of the street that led to the Gritti. The wind was at their backs and it blew the girl's hair forward. The wind parted her hair in the back and blew it forward about her face. They were looking in the shop windows and the girl stopped in front of the lighted window of a jewelry shop.

There were many good pieces of old jewelry in the window and they stood and looked at them and pointed out the best ones to each other, unclasping their hands to do so.

"Is there anything you really want? I could get it in the morning. Cipriani would loan me the money."

"No," she said. "I do not want anything but I notice that you never give me presents."

"You are much richer than I am. I bring you small things from the PX and I buy you drinks and meals."

"And take me in gondolas and to lovely places in the country."

"I never thought you wanted presents of hard stones."

"I don't. It is just the thought of giving and then one looks at them and thinks about them when they are worn."

"I'm learning," the Colonel said. "But what could I buy you on Army pay that would be like your square emeralds?"

"But don't you see. I inherited them. They came from my grandmother, and she had them from her mother who had them from her mother. Do you think it is the same to wear stones that come from dead people?"

"I never thought about it."

"You can have them if you like, if you like stones. To me they are only something to wear like a dress from Paris. You don't like to wear your dress uniform, do you?"

"No."

"You don't like to carry a sword, do you?"

"No, repeat, no."

"You are not that kind of a soldier and I am not that sort of girl. But sometime give me something lasting that I can wear and be happy each time I wear it."

"I see," the Colonel said. "And I will."

"You learn fast about things you do not know," the girl said. "And you make lovely quick decisions. I would like you to have the emeralds and you could keep them in your pocket like a lucky piece, and feel them if you were lonely."

"I don't put my hands much in my pockets when I'm working. I usually twirl a stick, or something, or point things out with a pencil."

"But you could put your hand in your pocket only once in a long time and feel them."

"I'm not lonely when I'm working. I have to think too hard to ever be lonely."

"But you are not working now."

"No. Only preparing the best way to be over-run."

"I'm going to give them to you anyway. I'm quite sure Mummy will understand. Also I won't need to tell her for quite a long time. She keeps no check on my things. I'm sure my maid would never tell her."

"I don't think I should take them."

"You should, please, to give me pleasure."

"I'm not sure it's honorable."

"That is like not being sure whether you are a virgin. What you do to give pleasure to another whom you love is most honorable."

"All right," the Colonel said. "I will take them for better or for worse."

"Now you say thank you," the girl said and slipped them into his pocket as quickly and ably as a jewel thief might. "I brought them with me because I have been thinking and deciding about this all week."

"I thought you thought about my hand."

"Don't be surly, Richard. And *you* should never be stupid. It is your hand you touch them with. Didn't you think of that?"

"No. And I was stupid. What would you like from that window?"

"I would like that small Negro with the ebony face and the turban made of chip diamonds with the small ruby on the crown of the turban. I should wear it as a pin. Everyone wore them in the old days in this city and the faces were those of their confidential servants. I have coveted this for a long time, but I wanted you to give it to me."

"I'll send it in the morning."

"No. Give it to me when we have lunch before you go."

"Right," the Colonel said.

"Now we must walk or we will be too late for dinner."

They started to walk, arm through arm, and as they went up the first bridge, the wind lashed at them.

When the twinge came, the Colonel said to himself, the hell with that.

"Richard," the girl said. "Put your hand in your pocket to please me and feel them."

The Colonel did.

"They feel wonderful," he said.

CHAPTER XI

THEY came in, out of the wind and the cold, through the main entrance of the Gritti Palace Hotel, into the light and warmth of the lobby.

"Good evening, Contessa," the concierge said. "Good evening, my Colonel. It must be cold outside."

"It is," the Colonel said, and did not add any of the rough or obscene phrases about the extent of the cold, or the force of the wind, that he could ordinarily have employed, for their mutual pleasure when speaking, alone, with the concierge.

As they entered the long hallway that led to the big stairs and to the elevator, leaving, on your right, the entrance to the bar, the doorway onto the Grand Canal, and the entrance to the dining room, the *Gran Maestro* came out of the bar.

He was wearing a formal white jacket, cut long, and

he smiled at them and said, "Good evening, my Countess. Good evening, my Colonel."

"*Gran Maestro*," the Colonel said.

The *Gran Maestro* smiled and, still bowing, said, "We are dining in the bar at the far end. There is no one here now in the winter time and the dining room is too big. I have saved your table. We have a very fine lobster if you would like him to commence with."

"Is he really fresh?"

"I saw him this morning when he came from the market in a basket. He was alive and a dark green and completely unfriendly."

"Would you like lobster, Daughter, to start your dinner?"

The Colonel was conscious of using the word, and so was the *Gran Maestro*, and so was the girl. But to each one it meant a different thing.

"I wanted to have him for you in case any *pescecani* came in. They are down now to gamble at the Lido. I was not trying to sell him."

"I would love some lobster," the girl said. "Cold, and with mayonnaise. The mayonnaise rather stiff." She said this in Italian.

"It isn't too expensive?" she said to the Colonel, seriously.

"*Ay hija mia*," the Colonel said.

"Feel in your right pocket," she said.

"I'll see that he is not too expensive," the *Gran Maestro* said. "Or I'll buy him myself. I could get him quite easily with a week's wages."

"Sold to TRUST," the Colonel said, this being the code designation of the task force occupying Trieste. "He only costs me a day's wages."

"Put your hand in your right hand pocket and feel very rich," the girl said.

The *Gran Maestro* had sensed this was a private joke and had gone; silently. He was happy about the girl, whom he respected and admired, and he was happy for his Colonel.

"I am rich," the Colonel said. "But if you tease me about them, I will give them back, and on the linen tablecloth, and in public."

He was teasing rough in his turn; throwing in the counter-attack without even thinking.

"No you won't," she said. "Because you love them already."

"I would take anything I love and throw it off the highest cliff you ever saw and not wait to hear it bounce."

"No, you wouldn't," the girl said. "You would not throw me off any high cliffs."

"No," the Colonel agreed. "And forgive me for talking badly."

"You didn't talk very badly and I didn't believe it anyway," the girl told him. "Now should I go to the women's room to comb my hair and make myself presentable, or should I come up to your room?"

"Which do you wish?"

"To come to your room, of course, and see how you live and how things are there."

"What about the hotel?"

"Everything is known in Venice anyway. But it is also known who my family are and that I am a good girl. Also they know it is you and it is I. We have some credit to exhaust."

"Good," the Colonel said. "By stairs or elevator?"

"By elevator," she said, and he heard the change in her voice. "You can call a boy or we can run it ourselves."

"We run it ourselves," the Colonel said. "I checked out on elevators long ago."

It was a good ride with a slight bump, and a rectification at the end, and the Colonel thought: Checked out, eh? You better be checked out again.

The corridor was now not simply beautiful, but exciting, and putting the key into the lock was not a simple process, but a rite.

"Here it is," the Colonel said when he swung the door open. "What there is of it."

"It is charming," the girl said. "But it is awfully cold with the windows open."

"I'll close them."

"No, please. Leave them open if you like it that way."

The Colonel kissed her and felt her wonderful, long, young, lithe and properly built body against his own body, which was hard and good, but beat-up, and as he kissed her he thought of nothing.

They kissed for a long time, standing straight, and kissing true, in the cold of the open windows that were onto the Grand Canal.

"Oh," she said. Then, "Oh."

"We owe nothing," the Colonel said. "Not a thing."

"Will you marry me and will we have the five sons?"

"I will! I will."

"The thing is that, would you?"

"Of course."

"Kiss me once again and make the buttons of your uniform hurt me but not too much."

They stood there and kissed each other true. "I have a disappointment for you, Richard," she said. "I have a disappointment about everything."

She said it as a flat statement and it came to the Colonel in the same way as a message came from one of the three battalions, when the battalion commander spoke the absolute truth and told you the worst.

"You are positive?"

"Yes."

"My poor Daughter," he said.

Now there was nothing dark about the word and she was his Daughter, truly, and he pitied her and loved her.

"No matter," he said. "You comb yourself and make a new mouth and all that, and we will have a good dinner."

"Say once more, first, that you love me and make the buttons very tight."

"I love you," the Colonel said quite formally.

Then he whispered into her ear as gently as he knew how to whisper, as his whisper was when they are fifteen feet away and you are a young lieutenant on a patrol, "I love you only, my best and last and only and one true love."

"Good," she said, and kissed him hard so he could feel the sweet salt of the blood inside his lip. And I like that too, he thought.

"Now I will comb my hair and make my mouth new and you can watch me."

"Do you want me to shut the windows?"

"No," she said. "We will do it all in the cold."

"Who do you love?"

"You," she said. "And we don't have too much luck do we?"

"I don't know," the Colonel said. "Go ahead and comb your hair."

The Colonel went into the bathroom to wash up for dinner. The bathroom was the only disappointing part of the room. Due to the exigencies of the Gritti having been built as a palace, there had been no site for bathrooms at the time of building, and, later, when they were introduced, they had been built down the corridor and those entitled to use them gave due warning before-hand and water was heated and towels laid out.

This bathroom had been cut, arbitrarily, from a corner of the room and it was a defensive, rather than an attacking bathroom, the Colonel felt. Washing, and forced to look in the mirror to check any traces of lipstick, he regarded his face.

It looks as though it had been cut out of wood by an indifferent craftsman, he thought.

He looked at the different welts and ridges that had come before they had plastic surgery, and at the thin, only to be observed by the initiate, lines of the excellent plastic operations after head wounds.

Well, that is what I have to offer as a *gueule* or a *façade*, he thought. It is a damn poor offer. The only thing is that it is tanned, and that takes some of the curse off of it. But, Christ what an ugly man.

He did not notice the old used steel of his eyes nor the small, long extending laugh wrinkles at the corners of his eyes, nor that his broken nose was like a gladiator's in the oldest statues. Nor did he notice his basically kind mouth which could be truly ruthless.

The hell with you, he said to the mirror. You beat-up, miserable. Should we rejoin the ladies?

He went out from the bathroom into the room, and he was as young as at his first attack. Every worthless thing had been left in the bathroom. As always, he thought. That's the place for it.

Où sont les neiges d'antan? Où sont les neiges d'autrefois? Dans le pissoir toute la chose comme ça.

The girl whose first name was Renata, had the doors of the tall armoire open. They were all mirrored inside and she was combing her hair.

She was not combing it for vanity, nor to do to the Colonel what she knew it could and would do. She was combing it with difficulty and without respect, and, since it was very heavy hair and as alive as the hair of peasants, or the hair of the beauties of the great nobility, it was resistant to the comb.

"The wind made it very tangled," she said. "Do you love me still?"

"Yes," the Colonel said. "May I help you?"

"No, I've done it all my life."

"You *could* stand sidewise."

"No. All contours are for our five sons and for your head to rest on."

"I was only thinking of the face," the Colonel said. "But thank you for calling my attention. My attention has been faulty again."

"I am over bold."

"No," the Colonel said. "In America, they make such things of wire and of sponge-rubber, such as you use in the seats of tanks. You never know there, whether there is any truth in the matter, unless you are a bad boy as I am."

"Here it is not that way," she said, and, with the comb, swung her now parted hair forward so that it came below the line of her cheek, and slanting back, hung over her shoulders.

"Do you like it neat?"

"It's not too neat but it is damn lovely."

"I could put it up and all that sort of thing if you value neatness. But I cannot manage hairpins and it seems so silly." Her voice was so lovely and it always reminded him of Pablo Casals playing the cello that it made him feel as a wound does that you think you cannot bear. But you can bear anything, he thought.

"I love you very much the way you are," the Colonel said. "And you are the most beautiful woman I have ever known, or seen, even in paintings by good painters."

"I wonder why the portrait has not come."

"The portrait is lovely to have," the Colonel said, and now he was a General again without thinking of it. "But it is like skinning a dead horse."

"Please don't be rough," the girl said. "I don't feel at all like being rough tonight."

"I slipped into the jargon of my *sale métier*."

"No," she said. "Please put your arms around me. Gently and well. Please. It is not a dirty trade. It is the oldest and the best, although most people who practice it are unworthy."

He held her as tight as he could without hurting and she said, "I would not have you be a lawyer nor a priest. Nor sell things. Nor be a great success. I love you to be in your trade and I love you. Please whisper to me if you wish."

The Colonel whispered; holding her tight, and with his heart broken, honestly and fairly, in his whisper that was as barely audible as a silent dog whistle heard close to the ear, "I love you, devil. And you're my Daughter, too. And I don't care about our losses because the moon is our mother and our father. And now let's go down to dinner."

He whispered this last so low that it was inaudible to anyone who did not love you.

"Yes," the girl said. "Yes. But kiss me once more first."

CHAPTER XII

THEY were at their table in the far corner of the bar, where the Colonel had both his flanks covered, and he rested solidly against the corner of the room. The *Gran Maestro* knew about this, since he had been an excellent sergeant in a good company of infantry, in a first-rate regiment, and he would no more have seated his Colonel in the middle of a room than he would have taken up a stupid defensive position.

"The lobster," the *Gran Maestro* said.

The lobster was imposing. He was double the size a lobster should be, and his unfriendliness had gone with the boiling, so that now he looked a monument to his dead self; complete with protruding eyes and his delicate, far-extended antennae that were for knowing what rather stupid eyes could not tell him.

He looks a little bit like Georgie Patton, the Colonel thought. But he probably never cried in his life when he was moved.

"Do you think that he will be tough?" he asked the girl in Italian.

"No," the *Gran Maestro* assured them, still bowing with the lobster. "He's truly not tough. He's only big. You know the type."

"All right," the Colonel said. "Serve him."

"And what will you drink?"

"What do you want, Daughter?"

"What you want."

"Capri Bianco," the Colonel said. "Secco and really cold."

"I have it ready," said the *Gran Maestro*.

"We are having fun," the girl said. "We are having it again and without sorrow. Isn't he an imposing lobster?"

"He is," the Colonel answered. "And he better damn well be tender."

"He will be," the girl told him. "The *Gran Maestro* doesn't lie. Isn't it wonderful to have people who do not lie?"

"Very wonderful and quite rare," the Colonel said. "I was thinking just now of a man named Georgie Patton who possibly never told the truth in his life."

"Do you ever lie?"

"I've lied four times. But each time I was very tired. That's not an excuse," he added.

"I lied a lot when I was a little girl. But mostly it was making up stories. Or I hope so. But I have never lied to my own advantage."

"I have," said the Colonel. "Four times."

"Would you have been a general if you had not lied?"

"If I had lied as others lied, I would have been a three-star general."

"Would it make you happier to be a three-star general?"

"No," said the Colonel. "It would not."

"Put your right hand, your real hand, in your pocket once and tell me how you feel."

The Colonel did so.

"Wonderful," he said. "But I have to give them back you know."

"No. Please no."

"We won't go into it now."

Just then the lobster was served.

It was tender, with the peculiar slippery grace of that kicking muscle which is the tail, and the claws were excellent; neither too thin, nor too fat.

"A lobster fills with the moon," the Colonel told the girl. "When the moon is dark he is not worth eating."

"I didn't know that."

"I think it may be because, with the full moon, he feeds all night. Or maybe it is that the full moon brings him feed."

"They come from the Dalmatian coast do they not?"

"Yes," the Colonel said. "That's your rich coast in fish. Maybe I should say *our* rich coast."

"Say it," the girl said. "You don't know how important things that are said are."

"They are a damn sight more important when you put them on paper."

117

"No," the girl said. "I don't agree. The paper means nothing unless you say them in your heart."

"And what if you haven't a heart, or your heart is worthless?"

"You have a heart and it is not worthless."

I would sure as hell like to trade it in on a new one, the Colonel thought. I do not see why that one, of all the muscles, should fail me. But he said nothing of this, and put his hand in his pocket.

"They feel wonderful," he said. "And you look wonderful."

"Thank you," she said. "I will remember that all week."

"You could always just look in the glass."

"The mirror bores me," she said. "Putting on lipstick and moving your mouths over each other to get it spread properly and combing your too heavy hair is not a life for a woman, or even a girl alone, who loves someone. When you want to be the moon and various stars and live with your man and have five sons, looking at yourself in the mirror and doing the artifices of a woman is not very exciting."

"Then let us be married at once."

"No," she said. "I had to make a decision about that, as about the other different things. All week long is my time to make decisions."

"I make them too," the Colonel told her. "But I am very vulnerable on this."

"Let's not talk about it. It makes a sweet hurt, but I think we would do better to find out what the *Gran*

Maestro has for meat. Please drink your wine. You haven't touched it."

"I'll touch it now," the Colonel said. He did and it was pale and cold like the wines of Greece, but not resinous, and its body was as full and as lovely as that of Renata.

"It's very like you."

"Yes. I know. That's why I wanted you to taste it."

"I'm tasting it," the Colonel said. "Now I will drink a full glass."

"You're a good man."

"Thank you," the Colonel said. "I'll remember that all week and try to be one." Then he said, "*Gran Maestro*."

When the *Gran Maestro* came over, happy, conspiratorial, and ignoring his ulcers, the Colonel asked him, "What sort of meat have you that is worth our eating?"

"I'm not quite sure I know," the *Gran Maestro* said. "But I will check. Your compatriot is over there in hearing distance. He would not let me seat him in the far corner."

"Good," the Colonel said. "We'll give him something to write about."

"He writes every night, you know. I've heard that from one of my colleagues at his hotel."

"Good," the Colonel said. "That shows that he is industrious even if he has outlived his talents."

"We are all industrious," the *Gran Maestro* said.

"In different ways."

"I will go and check on what there actually is among the meats."

"Check carefully."

"I am industrious."

"You are also damn sagacious."

The *Gran Maestro* was gone and the girl said, "He is a lovely man and I love how fond he is of you."

"We are good friends," the Colonel said. "I hope he has a good steak for you."

"There is one very good steak," the *Gran Maestro* said, reappearing.

"You take it, Daughter. I get them all the time at the mess. Do you want it rare?"

"Quite rare, please."

"*Al sangue*," the Colonel said, "as John said when he spoke to the waiter in French. *Crudo, bleu*, or just make it very rare."

"It's rare," the *Gran Maestro* said. "And you, my Colonel?"

"The scaloppine with Marsala, and the cauliflower braised with butter. Plus an artichoke vinaigrette if you can find one. What do you want, Daughter?"

"Mashed potatoes and a plain salad."

"You're a growing girl."

"Yes. But I should not grow too much nor in the wrong directions."

"I think that handles it," the Colonel said. "What about a fiasco of Valpolicella?"

"We don't have fiascos. This is a good hotel, you know. It comes in bottles."

"I forgot," the Colonel said. "Do you remember when it cost thirty centesimi the liter?"

"And we would throw the empty fiascos at the station guards from the troop trains?"

"And we would throw all the left over grenades away and bounce them down the hillside coming back from the Grappa?"

"And they would think there was a break-through when they would see the bursts and you never shaved, and we wore the *fiamme nere* on the grey, open jackets with the grey sweaters?"

"And I drank grappa and could not even feel the taste?"

"We must have been tough then," the Colonel said.

"We were tough then," the *Gran Maestro* said. "We were bad boys then, and you were the worst of the bad boys."

"Yes," the Colonel said. "I think we were rather bad boys. You forgive this will you, Daughter?"

"You haven't a picture of them, have you?"

"No. There weren't any pictures except with Mr. d'Annunzio in them. Also most of the people turned out badly."

"Except for us," the *Gran Maestro* said. "Now I must go and see how the steak marches."

The Colonel, who was a sub-lieutenant again now, riding in a camion, his face dust, until only his metallic eyes showed, and they were red-rimmed and sore, sat thinking.

The three key points, he thought. The massif of Grappa with Assalone and Pertica and the hill I do not remember the name of on the right. That was where I grew up, he thought, and all the nights I woke sweating, dreaming I would not be able to get them out of the trucks. They should not have gotten out, ever, of course. But what a trade it is.

"In our army, you know," he told the girl, "practically no Generals have ever fought. It is quite strange and the top organization dislikes those who have fought."

"Do Generals really fight?"

"Oh yes. When they are captains and lieutenants. Later, except in retreats, it is rather stupid."

"Did you fight much? I know you did. But tell me."

"I fought enough to be classified as a fool by the great thinkers."

"Tell me."

"When I was a boy, I fought against Erwin Rommel half way from Cortina to the Grappa, where we held. He was a captain then and I was an acting captain; really a sub-lieutenant."

"Did you know him?"

"No. Not until after the war when we could talk together. He was very nice and I liked him. We used to ski together."

"Did you like many Germans?"

"Very many. Ernst Udet I liked the best."

"But they were in the wrong."

"Of course. But who has not been?"

"I never could like them or take such a tolerant attitude as you do, since they killed my father and burned our villa on the Brenta and the day I saw a German officer shooting pigeons with a shot-gun in the Piazza San Marco."

"I understand," the Colonel said. "But please, Daughter, you try to understand my attitude too. When we have killed so many we can afford to be kind."

"How many have you killed?"

"One hundred and twenty-two sures. Not counting possibles."

"You had no remorse?"

"Never."

"Nor bad dreams about it?"

"Nor bad dreams. But usually strange ones. Combat dreams, always, for a while after combat. But then strange dreams about places mostly. We live by accidents of terrain, you know. And terrain is what remains in the dreaming part of your mind."

"Don't you ever dream about me?"

"I try to. But I can't."

"Maybe the portrait will help."

"I hope so," the Colonel said. "Please don't forget to remind me to give back the stones."

"Please don't be cruel."

"I have my small necessities of honor in the same proportions as we have our great and enveloping love. You cannot have the one without the other."

"But you could give me privileges."

"You have them," the Colonel said. "The stones are in my pocket."

The *Gran Maestro* came then with the steak and the scaloppine and the vegetables. They were brought by a sleek-headed boy who believed in nothing; but was trying hard to be a good second waiter. He was a member of the Order. The *Gran Maestro* served adroitly and with respect both for the food, and those that were to eat it.

"Now eat," he said.

"Uncork that Valpolicella," he said to the boy who had the eyes of an unbelieving spaniel.

"What do you have on that character?" the Colonel asked him, referring to his pitted compatriot, sitting chawing at his food, while the elderly woman with him ate with suburban grace.

"You should tell me. Not me you."

"I never saw him before today," the Colonel said. "He's hard to take with food."

"He condescends to me. He speaks bad Italian assiduously. He goes everywhere in Baedeker, and he has no taste in either food or wine. The woman is nice. I believe she is his aunt. But I have no real information."

"He looks like something we could do without."

"I believe we could. In a pinch."

"Does he speak of us?"

"He asked me who you were. He was familiar with the Contessa's name and had book-visited several palaces that had belonged to the family. He was impressed by your name, Madam, which I gave to impress him."

"Do you think he will put us in a book?"

"I'm sure of it. He puts everything in a book."

"We ought to be in a book," the Colonel said. "Would you mind, Daughter?"

"Of course not," the girl said. "But I'd rather Dante wrote it."

"Dante isn't around," the Colonel said.

"Can you tell me anything about the war?" the girl asked. "Anything that I should be permitted to know?"

"Sure. Anything you like."

"What was General Eisenhower like?"

"Strictly the Epworth League. Probably that is unjust too. Also complicated by various other influences. An excellent politician. Political General. Very able at it."

"The other leaders?"

"Let us not name them. They've named themselves enough in their memoirs. Mostly extremely plausible out of something called the Rotary Club that you would never have heard of. In this club, they have enameled buttons with their first names and you are fined if you call them by their proper names. Never fought. Ever."

"Were there no good ones?"

"Yes, many. Bradley, the schoolmaster, and many others. Give you Lightning Joe as a good one. Very good."

"Who was he?"

"Commanded the Seventh Corps when I was there. Very sound. Rapid. Accurate. Now chief of staff."

"But what about the great leaders we heard about like the Generals Montgomery and Patton?"

"Forget them, Daughter. Monty was a character who needed fifteen to one to move, and then moved tardily."

"I always supposed he was a great General."

"He was not," the Colonel said. "The worst part was he knew it. I have seen him come into an hotel and change from his proper uniform into a crowd-catching kit to go out in the evening to animate the populace."

"Do you dislike him?"

"No. I simply think he is a British General. Whatever that means. And don't you use the term."

"But he beat General Rommel."

"Yes. And you don't think any one else had softened him up? And who can't win with fifteen to one? When we fought here, when we were boys, the *Gran Maestro* and I, we won for one whole year with three to four against one and we won each one. Three main bad ones. That is why we can make jokes and not be solemn. We had something over one hundred and forty thousand dead that year. That is why we can speak gaily and without pomposity."

"It is such a sad science; if it is a science," the girl said. "I hate the war monuments, though I respect them."

"I do not like them either. Nor the process which led to their construction. Have you ever seen that end of the thing?"

"No. But I would like to know."

"Better not know," the Colonel said. "Eat your steak before it gets cold and forgive me for talking about my trade."

"I hate it but I love it."

"I believe we share the same emotions," the Colonel said. "But what is my pitted compatriot thinking three tables down?"

"About his next book, or about what it says in Bae-deker."

"Should we go and ride in a gondola in the wind after we have dined?"

"That would be lovely."

"Should we tell the pitted man that we are going? I think he has the same pits on his heart and in his soul and maybe in his curiosity."

"We tell him nothing," the girl said. "The *Gran Maestro* can convey him any information we wish."

Then she chewed well and solidly on her steak and said, "Do you think it is true that men make their own faces after fifty?"

"I hope not. Because I would not sign for mine."

"You," she said. "You."

"Is the steak good?" the Colonel asked.

"It's wonderful. How are your scaloppine?"

"Very tender and the sauce is not at all sweet. Do you like the vegetables?"

"The cauliflower is almost crisp; like celery."

"We should have some celery. But I don't think there is any or the *Gran Maestro* would have brought it."

"Don't we have fun with food? Imagine if we could eat together always."

"I've suggested it."

"Let's not talk about that."

"All right," the Colonel said. "I've made a decision too. I'm going to chuck the army and live in this town, very simply, on my retirement pay."

"That's wonderful. How do you look in civilian clothes?"

"You've seen me."

"I know it, my dear. I said it for a joke. You make rough jokes sometimes too, you know."

"I'll look all right. That is if you have a tailor here who can cut clothes."

"There isn't one here, but there is in Rome. Can we drive together to Rome to get the clothes?"

"Yes. And we will live outside the town at Viterbo and only go in for the fittings and for dinner in the evening. Then we'll drive back in the night."

"Will we see cinema people and speak about them with candour and perhaps not have a drink with them?"

"We'll see them by the thousands."

"Will we see them being married for the second and third time and then being blessed by the Pope?"

"If you go in for that kind of thing."

"I don't," the girl said. "That's one reason that I cannot marry you."

"I see," the Colonel said. "Thank you."

"But I will love you, whatever that means, and you and I know what it means very well, as long as either of us is alive and after."

"I don't think you can love very much after you, yourself, are dead," the Colonel said.

He started to eat the artichoke, taking a leaf at a time, and dipping them, heavy side down, into the deep saucer of *sauce vinaigrette*.

"I don't know whether you can either," the girl said. "But I will try. Don't you feel better to be loved?"

"Yes," the Colonel said. "I feel as though I were out on

some bare-assed hill where it was too rocky to dig, and the rocks all solid, but with nothing jutting, and no bulges, and all of a sudden instead of being there naked, I was armoured. Armoured and the eighty-eights not there."

"You should tell that to our writer friend with the craters of the moon face so he could write it tonight."

"I ought to tell it to Dante if he was around," the Colonel, suddenly gone as rough as the sea when a line squall comes up, said. "I'd tell him what I'd do if I were shifted, or ascended, into an armoured vehicle under such circumstances."

Just then the Barone Alvarito came into the dining room. He was looking for them and, being a hunter, he saw them instantly.

He came over to the table and kissed Renata's hand, saying, "*Ciao*, Renata." He was almost tall, beautifully built in his town clothes, and he was the shyest man the Colonel had ever known. He was not shy from ignorance, nor from being ill at ease, nor from any defect. He was basically shy, as certain animals are, such as the Bongo that you will never see in the jungle, and that must be hunted with dogs.

"My Colonel," he said. He smiled as only the truly shy can smile.

It was not the easy grin of the confident, nor the quick slashing smile of the extremely durable and the wicked. It had no relation with the poised, intently used smile of the courtesan or the politician. It was the strange, rare smile which rises from the deep, dark pit, deeper than a well, deep as a deep mine, that is within them.

"I can only stay a moment. I came to tell you that it looks quite good for the shoot. The ducks are coming in heavily from the north. There are many big ducks. The ones you like," he smiled again.

"Sit down Alvarito. Please."

"No," the Barone Alvarito said. "We can meet at the Garage at two-thirty if you like? You have your car?"

"Yes."

"That makes it very good. Leaving at that hour, we will have time to see the ducks in the evening."

"Splendid," the Colonel said.

"*Ciao*, then, Renata. Good-bye, my Colonel. Until two-thirty."

"We knew each other as children," the girl said. "But he was about three years older. He was born very old."

"Yes. I know. He is a good friend of mine."

"Do you think your compatriot has looked him up in Baedeker?"

"I wouldn't know," the Colonel said. "*Gran Maestro*," he asked, "did my illustrious compatriot look up the *Barone* in Baedeker?"

"Truly, my Colonel. I have not seen him pull his Baedeker during the meal."

"Give him full marks," the Colonel said. "Now look. I believe that the Valpolicella is better when it is newer. It is not a *grand vin* and bottling it and putting years on it only adds sediment. Do you agree?"

"I agree."

"Then what should we do?"

130

"My Colonel, you know that in a Great Hotel, wine must cost money. You cannot get Pinard at the Ritz. But I suggest that we get several fiascos of the good. You can say they come from the Contessa Renata's estates and are a gift. Then I will have them decanted for you. This way, we will have better wine and make an impressive saving. I will explain it to the manager if you like. He is a very good man."

"Explain it to him," the Colonel said. "He's not a man who drinks labels either."

"Agreed."

"In the meantime you might as well drink this. It is very good, you know."

"It is," the Colonel said. "But it isn't *Chambertin*."

"What did we use to drink?"

"Anything," the Colonel said. "But now I seek perfection. Or, rather, not absolute perfection, but perfection for my money."

"I seek it, too," the *Gran Maestro* said. "But rather vainly."

"What do you want for the end of the meal?"

"Cheese," the Colonel said. "What do you want, Daughter?"

The girl had been quiet and a little withdrawn, since she had seen Alvarito. Something was going on in her mind, and it was an excellent mind. But, momentarily, she was not with them.

"Cheese," she said. "Please."

"What cheese?"

"Bring them all and we'll look at them," the Colonel said.

The *Gran Maestro* left and the Colonel said, "What's the matter, Daughter?"

"Nothing. Never anything. Always nothing."

"You might as well pull out of it. We haven't time for such luxuries."

"No. I agree. We will devote ourselves to the cheese."

"Do I have to take it like a corn cob?"

"No," she said, not understanding the colloquialism, but understanding exactly what was meant, since it was she who had been doing the thinking. "Put your right hand in your pocket."

"Good," the Colonel said. "I will."

He put his right hand in his pocket and felt what was there, first with the tips of his fingers, and then with the insides of his fingers, and then with the palm of his hand; his split hand.

"I'm sorry," she said. "And now we begin the good part of it again. We will dedicate ourselves to the cheese with happiness."

"Excellent," the Colonel said. "I wonder what cheeses he has?"

"Tell me about the last war," the girl said. "Then we will ride in our gondola in the cold wind."

"It was not very interesting," the Colonel said. "To us, of course, such things are always interesting. But there were only three, maybe four, phases that really interested me."

"Why?"

"We were fighting a beaten enemy whose communications had been destroyed. We destroyed many divisions on paper, but they were ghost divisions. Not real ones. They had been destroyed by our tactical aviation before they ever got up. It was only really difficult in Normandy, due to the terrain, and when we made the break for Georgie Patton's armour to go through and held it open on both sides."

"How do you make a break for armour to go through? Tell me, please."

"First you fight to take a town that controls all the main roads. Call the town St. Lo. Then you have to open up the roads by taking other towns and villages. The enemy has a main line of resistance, but he cannot bring up his divisions to counter-attack because the fighter-bombers catch them on the roads. Does this bore you? It bores the hell out of me."

"It does not bore me. I never heard it said understandably before."

"Thank you," the Colonel said. "Are you sure you want more of the sad science?"

"Please," she said. "I love you, you know, and I would like to share it with you."

"Nobody shares this trade with anybody," the Colonel told her. "I'm just telling you how it works. I can insert anecdotes to make it interesting, or plausible."

"Insert some, please."

"The taking of Paris was nothing," the Colonel said. "It was only an emotional experience. Not a military operation. We killed a number of typists and the screen the Germans had left, as they always do, to cover their withdrawal. I suppose they figured they were not going to need a hell of a lot of office workers any more and they left them as soldiers."

"Was it not a great thing?"

"The people of Leclerc, another jerk of the third or fourth water, whose death I celebrated with a magnum of Perrier-Jouet Brut 1942, shot a great number of rounds to make it seem important and because we had given them what they had to shoot with. But it was not important."

"Did you take part in it?"

"Yes," the Colonel said. "I think I could safely say, yes."

"Did you have no great impressions of it? After all, it was Paris and not everyone has taken it."

"The French, themselves, had taken it four days before. But the grand plan of what we called SHAEF, Supreme, get that word, Headquarters of the Allied Expeditionary Forces, which included all the military politicians of the rear, and who wore a badge of shame in the form of a flaming something, while we wore a four-leafed clover as a designation, and for luck, had a master plan for the envelopment of the city. So we could not simply take it.

"Also we had to wait for the possible arrival of General or Field Marshal Bernard Law Montgomery who was unable to close, even, the gap at Falaise and found the going rather sticky and could not quite get there on time."

"You must have missed him," the girl said.

"Oh, we did," the Colonel said. "No end."

"But was there nothing noble or truly happy about it?"

"Surely," the Colonel told her. "We fought from Bas Meudon, and then the Porte de Saint Cloud, through streets I knew and loved and we had no deads and did as little damage as possible. At the Etoile I took Elsa Maxwell's butler prisoner. It was a very complicated operation. He had been denounced as a Japanese sniper. A new thing. Several Parisians were alleged to have been killed by him. So we sent three men to the roof where he had taken refuge and he was an Indo-China boy."

"I begin to understand a little. But it is disheartening."

"It is always disheartening as hell. But you are not supposed to have a heart in this trade."

"But do you think it was the same in the time of the Grand Captains?"

"I am quite sure it was worse."

"But you got your hand honorably?"

"Yes. Very honorably. On a rocky, bare-assed hill."

"Please let me feel it," she said.

"Just be careful around the center," the Colonel said. "It's split there and it still cracks open."

"You ought to write," the girl said. "I mean it truly. So someone would know about such things."

"No," the Colonel disagreed. "I have not the talent for it and I know too much. Almost any liar writes more convincingly than a man who was there."

"But other soldiers wrote."

"Yes. Maurice de Saxe. Frederick the Great. Mr. T'sun Su."

"But soldiers of our time."

"You use the word our with facility. I like it though."

"But didn't many modern soldiers write?"

"Many. But did you ever read them?"

"No. I have read mostly the classics and I read the illustrated papers for the scandals. Also, I read your letters."

"Burn them," the Colonel said. "They are worthless."

"Please. Don't be rough."

"I won't. What can I tell you that won't bore you?"

"Tell me about when you were a General."

"Oh, that," he said and motioned to the *Gran Maestro* to bring Champagne. It was Roederer Brut '42 and he loved it.

"When you are a general you live in a trailer and your Chief of Staff lives in a trailer, and you have bourbon whisky when other people do not have it. Your G's live in the C.P. I'd tell you what G's are, but it would bore you. I'd tell you about G1, G2, G3, G4, G5 and on the other side there is always Kraut-6. But it would bore you. On the other hand, you have a map covered with plastic material, and on this you have three regiments composed of three battalions each. It is all marked in colored pencil.

"You have boundary lines so that when the battalions cross their boundaries they will not then fight each other. Each battalion is composed of five companies. All should be good, but some are good, and some are not so good. Also you have divisional artillery and a battalion of tanks and many spare parts. You live by co-ordinates."

He paused while the *Gran Maestro* poured the Roederer Brut '42.

"From Corps," he translated, unlovingly, *cuerpo d'Armata*, "they tell you what you must do, and then you decide how to do it. You dictate the orders or, most often, you give them by telephone. You ream out people you respect, to make them do what you know is fairly impossible, but is ordered. Also, you have to think hard, stay awake late and get up early."

"And you won't write about this? Not even to please me?"

"No," said the Colonel. "Boys who were sensitive and cracked and kept all their valid first impressions of their day of battle, or their three days, or even their four, write books. They are good books but can be dull if you have been there. Then others write to profit quickly from the war they never fought in. The ones who ran back to tell the news. The news is hardly exact. But they ran quickly with it. Professional writers who had jobs that prevented them from fighting wrote of combat that they could not understand, as though they had been there. I do not know what category of sin that comes under.

"Also a nylon-smooth Captain of the Navy who could not command a cat-boat wrote about the intimate side of the truly Big Picture. Everybody will write their book sooner or later. We might even draw a good one. But I don't write, Daughter."

He motioned for the *Gran Maestro* to fill the glasses.

"*Gran Maestro*," he said. "Do you like to fight?"

"No."

"But we fought?"

"Yes. Too much."

"How is your health?"

"Wonderful except for the ulcers and a small cardiac condition."

"No," the Colonel said, and his heart rose and he felt it choke him. "You only told me about the ulcers."

"Well you know now," the *Gran Maestro* said and did not finish the sentence and he smiled his best and clearest smile that came as solid as the sun rises.

"How many times?"

The *Gran Maestro* held up two fingers as a man might do giving odds where he had credit, and all the betting was on the nod.

"I'm ahead of you," the Colonel said. "But let's not be macabre. Ask Donna Renata if she wishes more of this excellent wine."

"You did not tell me there were more," the girl said. "You owe it to me to tell me."

"There has been nothing since we were together last."

"Do you think it breaks for me? If so, I would come and simply be with you and care for you."

"It's just a muscle," the Colonel said. "Only it is the main muscle. It works as perfectly as a Rolex Oyster Perpetual. The trouble is you cannot send it to the Rolex representative when it goes wrong. When it stops, you just do not know the time. You're dead."

"Don't please talk about it."

"You asked me," the Colonel said.

"And that pitted man with the caricature face? He has no such thing?"

"Of course not," the Colonel told her. "If he is a mediocre writer he will live forever."

"But you're not a writer. How do you know this?"

"No," the Colonel said. "By the grace of God. But I've read several books. We have a lot of time to read when we are unmarried. Not as much as the merchant marine maybe. But plenty. I can tell one writer from another and I tell you that a mediocre writer has a long span of life. They ought to all draw longevity pay."

"Could you tell me any anecdotes, and we stop talking about this, which is my true sorrow?"

"I can tell you hundreds of them. All true."

"Tell me just one. Then we will finish this wine and then go in the gondola."

"Do you think you will be warm enough?"

"Oh, I'm sure I will."

"I don't know what to tell you," the Colonel said. "Everything about war bores those who have not made it. Except the tales of the liars."

"I would like to know about the taking of Paris."

"Why? Because I told you that you looked like Marie Antoinette in the tumbril?"

"No. I was complimented by that and I know we are a little alike in profile. But I have never been in any tumbril, and I would like to hear about Paris. When you love someone and he is your hero, you like to hear about the places and the things."

"Please turn your head," the Colonel said, "and I will

tell you. *Gran Maestro* is there any more in that wretched bottle?"

"No," the *Gran Maestro* answered.

"Then bring another."

"I have one already iced."

"Good. Serve it. Now, Daughter, we parted from the column of the General Leclerc at Clamart. They went to Montrouge and the Porte d'Orleans and we went directly to Bas Meudon and secured the bridge of the Porte de Saint Cloud. Is this too technical and does it bore you?"

"No."

"It would be better with a map."

"Go on."

"We secured the bridge and established a bridge-head on the other side of the river and we threw the Germans, living and dead, who had defended the bridge, into the Seine River," he stopped. "It was a token defense of course. They should have blown it. We threw all these Germans into the River Seine. They were nearly all office workers, I believe."

"Go on."

"The next morning, we were informed that the Germans had strong points at various places, and artillery on Mount Valérien, and that tanks were roaming the streets. A portion of this was true. We were also requested not to enter too rapidly as the General Leclerc was to take the city. I complied with this request and entered as slowly as I could."

"How do you do that?"

"You hold up your attack two hours and you drink

champagne whenever it is offered to you by patriots, collaborators or enthusiasts."

"But was there nothing wonderful nor great, the way it is in books?"

"Of course. There was the city itself. The people were very happy. Old general officers were walking about in their moth-balled uniforms. We were very happy, too, not to have to fight."

"Did you not have to fight at all?"

"Only three times. Then not seriously."

"But was that all you had to fight to take such a city?"

"Daughter, we fought twelve times from Rambouillet to enter the city. But only two of them were worth describing as fights. Those at Toussus le Noble and at LeBuc. The rest was the necessary garnishing of a dish. I really did not need to fight at all except at those two places."

"Tell me some true things about fighting."

"Tell me you love me."

"I love you," the girl said. "You can publish it in the Gazzettino if you like. I love your hard, flat body and your strange eyes that frighten me when they become wicked. I love your hand and all your other wounded places."

"I better try to tell you something pretty good," the Colonel said. "First I can tell you that I love you Period."

"Why don't you buy some good glass?" the girl asked, suddenly. "We could go to Murano together."

"I don't know anything about glass."

"I could teach you. It would be fun."

"We lead too nomadic a life for good glass."

"But when you retire and live here."

"We'll get some then."

"I wish that that was now."

"So do I, except that I go duck shooting tomorrow and that tonight is tonight."

"Can I come duck shooting?"

"Only if Alvarito asks you."

"I can make him ask me."

"I doubt that."

"It isn't polite to doubt what your Daughter says when she is old enough not to lie."

"All right, Daughter. I withdraw the doubt."

"Thank you. For that I will not go and be a nuisance. I will stay in Venice and go to Mass with Mother and my aunt and my great-aunt and visit my poors. I am an only child so I have many duties."

"I always wondered what you did."

"That's what I do. Also, I'll have my maid wash my head and give me a manicure and a pedicure."

"You can't do that because the shoot is on Sunday."

"Then I'll do that on Monday. On Sunday, I will read all the illustrated papers including the outrageous ones."

"Maybe they'll have pictures of Miss Bergman. Do you still want to be like her?"

"Not any more," the girl said. "I want to be like me only much, much better and I want to have you love me."

"Also," she said suddenly and unmaskingly, "I want to be like you. Can I be like you a little while tonight?"

"Of course," the Colonel said. "In what town are we anyway?"

"Venice," she said. "The best town, I think."

"I quite agree. And thank you for not asking me for more war episodes."

"Oh you are going to have to tell them to me later."

"*Have to?*" the Colonel said and the cruelty and resolution showed in his strange eyes as clearly as when the hooded muzzle of the gun of a tank swings toward you.

"Did you say *have to*, Daughter?"

"I said it. But I did not mean it in that way. Or, if I did wrong, I am sorry. I meant will you please tell me more true episodes later? And explain me the things I do not understand?"

"You can use *have to* if you want, Daughter. The hell with it."

He smiled and his eyes were as kind as they ever were, which was not too kind, as he knew. But there was nothing now that he could do about it except to try to be kind to his last and true and only love.

"I don't really mind, Daughter. Please believe me. I know about command and, at your age, I used to take considerable pleasure in exercising it."

"But I don't want to command," the girl said. In spite of her resolution not to cry, her eyes were wet. "I wish to serve you."

"I know. But you wish to command, too. There's nothing wrong in that. All people such as us have it."

"Thank you for the such as us."

143

"It wasn't hard to say," the Colonel said. "Daughter," he added.

Just then the concierge came to the table and said, "Excuse me, my Colonel. There is a man outside, I believe he is a servant of yours, my Lady, with quite a large package which he says is for the Colonel. Should I keep it in the storeroom or have it sent to your room?"

"To my room," the Colonel said.

"Please," the girl said. "Can't we look at it here? We don't care about anyone here, do we?"

"Have it unwrapped and brought in here."

"Very good."

"Later, you may have it taken with great care to my room and have it wrapped, solidly, for transport at noon tomorrow."

"Very good, my Colonel."

"Are you excited to see it?" the girl asked.

"Very," said the Colonel. "*Gran Maestro* some more of that Roederer, please, and please place a chair in such a position that we may view a portrait. We are devotees of the pictorial arts."

"There's no more Roederer cold," the *Gran Maestro* said. "But if you would like some Perrier-Jouet—"

"Bring it," the Colonel said and added, "Please."

"I don't talk like Georgie Patton," the Colonel told her. "I don't have to. And besides he's dead."

"Poor man."

"Yes, Poor man all his life. Although quite rich in money and with a lot of armour."

"Do you have anything against armour?"

"Yes. Most of the people inside of it. It makes men into bullies which is the first step toward cowardice; true cowardice I mean. Perhaps it is a little complicated by claustrophobia."

Then he looked at her and smiled and regretted taking her beyond her depth, as you might take a new swimmer on a shallow, shelving beach, into too deep water; and he sought to reassure her.

"You forgive me, Daughter. Much of what I say is unjust. But it is truer than the things that you will read in Generals' memoirs. After a man gets one star, or more, the truth becomes as difficult for him to attain as the Holy Grail was in our ancestors' time."

"But you were a general officer."

"Not for too damn long," the Colonel said. "Now Captains," the General said, "they know the exact truth and they can mostly tell it to you. If they can't, you reclassify them."

"Would you reclassify me if I lied?"

"It would depend on what you lied about."

"I'm not going to lie about anything. I don't want to be reclassified. It sounds horrible."

"It is," the Colonel said. "And you send them back to have it done to them with eleven different copies of why it should be done, every one of which you sign."

"Did you reclassify many?"

"Plenty."

The concierge came into the room with the portrait,

carrying it in its big frame, much as a ship moves when she is carrying too much sail.

"Get two chairs," the Colonel said to the second waiter, "and put them there. See that the canvas does not touch the chairs. And hold it so it does not slip."

Then to the girl he said, "We'll have to change that frame."

"I know," she said. "It was not my choice. Take it unframed with you and we'll choose a good frame next week. Now look at it. Not at the frame. At what it says, or does not say, of me."

It was a beautiful portrait; neither cold, nor snobbish, nor stylised, nor modern. It was the way you would want your girl painted if Tintoretto were still around and, if he were not around, you settled for Velasquez. It was not the way either of them painted. It was simply a splendid portrait painted, as they sometimes are, in our time.

"It's wonderful," the Colonel said. "It is truly lovely."

The concierge and the second waiter were holding it, and looking at it around the edges. The *Gran Maestro* was admiring fully. The American, two tables down, was looking at it with his journalistic eyes, wondering who painted it. The back of the canvas was to the other diners.

"It is wonderful," the Colonel said. "But you can't give me that."

"I already have," the girl said. "I'm sure my hair was never that long over my shoulders."

"I think it probably was."

"I could try to let it get that long if you want."

146

"Try," the Colonel said. "You great beauty you. I love you very much. You and you portrayed on canvas."

"Tell the waiters if you like. I'm sure it won't come as a great shock to them."

"Take the canvas upstairs to my room," the Colonel said to the concierge. "Thank you very much for bringing it in. If the price is right, I am going to buy it."

"The price is right," the girl said to him. "Should we have them take it and the chairs down and make a special showing of it for your compatriot? The *Gran Maestro* could tell him the address of the painter and he could visit the picturesque studio."

"It is a very lovely portrait," the *Gran Maestro* said. "But it should be taken to the room. One should never let Roederer or Perrier-Jouet do the talking."

"Take it to the room, please."

"You said please without a pause before it."

"Thank you," the Colonel said. "I am very deeply moved by the portrait and I am not entirely responsible for what I say."

"Let's neither of us be responsible."

"Agreed," the Colonel said. "The *Gran Maestro* is really very responsible. He always was."

"No," the girl said. "I think he did not only from responsibility but from malice. We all have malice, you know, of some kind or another in this town. I think perhaps he did not want the man to have even a journalist's look into happiness."

"Whatever that is."

"I learned that phrase from you, and now you have re-learned it back from me."

"That's the way it goes," the Colonel said. "What you win in Boston you lose in Chicago."

"I don't understand that at all."

"Too hard to explain," the Colonel said. Then, "No. Of course it isn't. Making things clear is my main trade. The hell with being too hard to explain. It is like professional football, *calcio*, What you win in Milano you lose in Torino."

"I don't care about football."

"Neither do I," the Colonel said. "Especially not about the Army and Navy game and when the very high brass speaks in terms of American football so they can understand, themselves, what they are talking of."

"I think we will have a good time tonight. Even under the circumstances, whatever they are."

"Should we take this new bottle in the gondola?"

"Yes," the girl said. "But with deep glasses. I'll tell the *Gran Maestro*. Let's get our coats and go."

"Good. I'll take some of this medicine and sign for the G.M. and we'll go."

"I wish it was me taking the medicine instead of you."

"I'm glad as hell it isn't," the Colonel said. "Should we pick our gondola or have them bring one to the landing?"

"Let's gamble and have them bring one to the landing. What do we have to lose?"

"Nothing, I guess. Probably nothing."

CHAPTER XIII

THEY went out the side door of the hotel to the *imbarcadero* and the wind hit them. The light from the hotel shone on the blackness of the gondola and made the water green. She looks as lovely as a good horse or as a racing shell, the Colonel thought. Why have I never seen a gondola before? What hand or eye framed that dark-ed symmetry?

"Where should we go?" the girl asked.

Her hair, in the light from the hotel door and window, as she stood on the dock by the black gondola, was blowing back in the wind, so she looked like the figure-head on a ship. The rest of it, too, the Colonel thought.

"Let's just ride through the park," the Colonel said. "Or through the Bois with the top down. Let him take us out to Armenonville."

"Will we go to Paris?"

"Sure," the Colonel said. "Tell him to take us for an

hour where the going is easiest. I don't want to drive him into that wind."

"The tide is quite high with this wind," the girl said. "Some of our places he couldn't get under the bridges. May I tell him where to go?"

"Of course, Daughter."

"Stow that ice bucket aboard," the Colonel said to the second waiter, who had come out with them.

"The *Gran Maestro* said to tell you, as you embarked, that this bottle of wine was his present."

"Thank him properly and tell him he can't do that."

"He had better go into the wind a little first," the girl said. "Then I know how he should go."

"The *Gran Maestro* sent this," the second waiter said.

It was a folded, old U. S. O. D. blanket. Renata was talking to the gondoliere, her hair blowing. The gondoliere wore a heavy blue navy sweater and he was bare-headed too.

"Thank him," the Colonel said.

He slipped a bill into the second waiter's hand. The second waiter returned it. "You already made the notation on the check. Neither you nor I nor the *Gran Maestro* are starving."

"What about the moglie and the bambini?"

"I don't have that. Your mediums smacked our house in Treviso."

"I'm sorry."

"You needn't be," the second waiter said. "You were a foot soldier as I was."

"Permit me to be sorry."

"Sure," the second waiter said. "And what the hell difference does it make? Be happy, my Colonel, and be happy, my Lady."

They got down into the gondola and there was the same magic, as always, of the light hull, and the sudden displacement that you made, and then the trimming in the dark privacy, and then the second trimming, as the *gondoliere* started to scull, laying her partly on her side so that he would have more control.

"Now," the girl said. "We are in our home and I love you. Please kiss me and put all love into it."

The Colonel held her close, with her head thrown back and kissed her until there was nothing left of the kiss but desperation.

"I love you."

"Whatever that means," she interrupted.

"I love you and I know whatever that means. The picture is lovely. But there is no word for what you are."

"Wild?" she said. "Or careless or unkempt?"

"No."

"The last was one of the first words I learned from my governess. It means you do not comb your hair enough. Neglectful is when you do not brush one hundred strokes at night."

"I'm going to run my hand through it and make it unkempter still."

"Your hurt hand?"

"Yes."

"We're sitting on the wrong sides for that. Change over."

"Good. That is a sensible order couched in simple language and easily understood."

It was fun moving over, trying not to disturb the balance of the gondola, but having to trim again carefully.

"Now," she said. "But hold me tightly with the other arm."

"You know just what you want?"

"I do indeed. Is it un-maidenly? I learned that word too from my governess."

"No," he said. "It's lovely. Pull up the blanket good and feel that wind."

"It's from the high mountains."

"Yes. And beyond there it's from somewhere else."

The Colonel heard the slap of the waves, and he felt the wind come sharply, and the rough familiarity of the blanket, and then he felt the girl cold-warm and lovely and with upraised breasts that his left hand coasted lightly over. Then he ran his bad hand through her hair once, twice, and three times and then he kissed her, and it was worse than desperation.

"Please," she said, from almost underneath the blanket. "Let me kiss now."

"No," he said. "Me again."

The wind was very cold and lashed their faces but under the blanket there was no wind nor nothing; only his ruined hand that searched for the island in the great river with the high steep banks.

"That's it," she said.

He kissed her then and he searched for the island, finding it and losing it, and then finding it for good. For good and for bad, he thought, and for good and for all.

"My darling," he said. "My well beloved. Please."

"No. Just hold me very tight and hold the high ground, too."

The Colonel said nothing, because he was assisting, or had made an act of presence, at the only mystery that he believed in except the occasional bravery of man.

"Please don't move," the girl said. "Then move a great amount."

The Colonel, lying under the blanket in the wind, knowing it is only what man does for woman that he retains, except what he does for his fatherland or his motherland, however you get the reading, proceeded.

"Please darling," the girl said. "I don't think I can stand it."

"Don't think of anything. Don't think of anything at all."

"I'm not."

"Don't think."

"Oh please let's not talk."

"Is it right?"

"You know."

"You're sure."

"Oh please not talk. Please."

Yes, he thought. Please and please again.

She said nothing, and neither did he, and when the great bird had flown far out of the closed window of the gondola, and was lost and gone, neither of them said anything. He held her head lightly with his good arm and the other arm held the high ground now.

"Please put it where it should be," she said. "Your hand."

"Should we?"

"No. Just hold me tight and try to love me true."

"I love you true," he said, and just then the gondola turned to the left, quite sharply, and the wind was on his right cheek, and he said, with his old eyes catching the outline of the Palace where they turned, and noting it, "You're in the lee now, Daughter."

"But it is too soon now. Don't you know how a woman feels?"

"No. Only what you tell me."

"Thank you for the you. But don't you really know?"

"No. I never asked, I guess."

"Guess now," she said. "And please wait until after we have gone under the second bridge."

"Take a glass of this," the Colonel said, reaching accurately and well for the champagne bucket with the ice, and uncorking the bottle the *Gran Maestro* had uncorked, and then placed a common wine cork in.

"This is good for you, Daughter. It is good for all the ills that all of us have, and for all sadness and indecision."

"I have none of those," she said, speaking grammatically as her governess had taught her. "I am just a woman, or a girl, or whatever that is, doing whatever it is she should not do. Let's do it again, please, now I am in the lee."

"Where is the island now and in what river?"

"You are making the discovery. I am only the unknown country."

"Not too unknown," the Colonel said.

"Please don't be rude," the girl said. "And please attack gently and with the same attack as before."

"It's no attack," the Colonel said. "It is something else."

"Whatever it is, whatever it is, while I'm still in the lee."

"Yes," the Colonel said. "Yes, now if you want, or will accept from kindness."

"Please, yes."

She talks like a gentle cat, though the poor cats cannot speak, the Colonel thought. But then he stopped thinking and he did not think for a long time.

The gondola now was in one of the secondary canals. When it had turned from the Grand Canal, the wind had swung it so the *gondoliere* had to shift all his weight as ballast, and the Colonel and the girl had shifted too, under the blanket, with the wind getting under the edge of the blanket; wildly.

They had not spoken for a long time and the Colonel had noted that the gondola had only inches free in passing under the last bridge.

"How are you, Daughter?"

"I'm quite lovely."

"Do you love me?"

"Please don't ask such silly things."

"The tide is very high and we only just made that last bridge."

"I think I know where we are going. I was born here."

"I've made mistakes in my home town," the Colonel said. "Being born there isn't everything."

"It is very much," the girl said. "You know that. Please hold me very tightly so we can be a part of each other for a little while·

"We can try," the Colonel said.

"Couldn't I be you?"

"That's awfully complicated. We could try of course."

"I'm you now," she said. "And I just took the city of Paris."

"Jesus, Daughter," he said. "You've got an awful lot of problems on your hands. The next thing, they will parade the twenty-eighth division through."

"I don't care."

"I do."

"Were they not good?"

"Sure. They had fine commanders, too. But they were National Guard and hard luck. What you call a T.S. division. Get your T.S. slip from the Chaplain."

"I understand none of those things."

"They aren't worth explaining," the Colonel said.

"Will you tell me some true things about Paris? I love it so much and when I think of you taking it, then, it is as though I were riding in this gondola with Maréchal Ney."

"A no good job," the Colonel said. "Anyway, not after

he fought all those rear-guard actions coming back from that big Russian town. He used to fight ten, twelve, fifteen times a day. Maybe more. Afterwards, he couldn't recognize people. Please don't get in any gondolas with him."

"He was always one of my great heroes."

"Yeah. Mine too. Until Quatre Bras. Maybe it wasn't Quatre Bras. I'm getting rusty. Give it the generic title of Waterloo."

"Was he bad there?"

"Awful," the Colonel told her. "Forget it. Too many rear-guard actions coming back from Moskova."

"But they called him the bravest of the brave."

"You can't eat on that. You have to be that, always, and then be the smartest of the smart. Then you need a lot of stuff coming up."

"Tell me about Paris, please. We should not make more love, I know."

"I don't know it. Who says it?"

"I say it because I love you."

"All right. You said it and you love me. So we act on that. The hell with it."

"Do you think we could once more if it would not hurt you?"

"Hurt me?" the Colonel said. "When the hell was I ever hurt?"

CHAPTER XIV

"PLEASE don't be bad," she said, pulling the blanket over them both. "Please drink a glass of this with me. You know you've been hurt."

"Exactly," the Colonel said. "Let's forget it."

"All right," she said. "I learned that word, or those two words from you. We have forgotten it."

"Why do you like the hand?" the Colonel asked, placing it where he should.

"Please don't pretend to be stupid, and please let's not think of anything, or anything, or anything."

"I am stupid," the Colonel said. "But I won't think of anything or anything nor of nothing nor of his brother, tomorrow."

"Please be good and kind."

"I will be. And I will tell you, now, a military secret. Top Secret equals British Most Secret. I love you."

"That's nice," she said. "And you put it nicely."

"I'm nice," the Colonel said, and checked on the bridge that was coming up, and saw there was clearance. "That's the first thing people notice about me."

"I always use the wrong words," the girl said. "Please just love me. I wish it was me who could love you."

"You do."

"Yes, I do," she said. "With all my heart."

They were going with the wind now and they were both tired.

"Do you think—"

"I don't think," the girl said.

"Well try and think."

"I will."

"Drink a glass of this."

"Why not? It's very good."

It was. There was still ice in the bucket, and the wine was cold and clear.

"Can I stay at the Gritti?"

"No."

"Why not?"

"It wouldn't be right. For them. Nor you. The hell with me."

"Then I suppose I should go home."

"Yes," the Colonel said. "That is the logical supposition."

"That is an awful way to say a sad thing. Can't we even pretend some things?"

"No. I'll take you home and you sleep good and well and tomorrow we will meet where and when you say."

"May I call the Gritti?"

"Of course. I'll always be awake. Will you call when you are awake?"

"Yes. But why do you always wake so early?"

"It is a business habit."

"Oh, I wish you were not in that business, and that you were not going to die."

"So do I," said the Colonel. "But I'm getting out of the business."

"Yes," she said, sleepily and comfortably. "Then we go to Rome and get the clothes."

"And live happily ever after."

"Please don't," she said. "Please, please, don't. You know I made the resolution not to cry."

"You're crying now," the Colonel said. "What the hell have you got to lose on that resolution?"

"Take me home please."

"That's what I was doing in the first place," the Colonel told her.

"Be kind once first."

"I will," the Colonel said.

After they, or the Colonel, rather, had paid the *gondoliere* who was unknowing, yet knowing all, solid, sound, respectful and trustworthy, they walked into the Piazzetta and then across the great, cold, wind-swept square that was hard and old under their feet. They walked holding close and hard in their sorrow and their happiness.

"This is the place where the German shot the pigeons," the girl said.

"We probably killed him," the Colonel said. "Or his

brother. Maybe we hanged him. I wouldn't know. I'm not in C.I.D."

"Do you love me still on these water-worn, cold and old stones?"

"Yes. I'd like to spread a bed roll here and prove it."

"That would be more barbarous than the pigeon shooter."

"I'm barbarous," the Colonel said.

"Not always."

"Thank you for the not always."

"We turn here."

"I think I know that. When are they going to tear that damned Cinema Palace down and put up a real cathedral? That's what T5 Jackson wants."

"When some one brings Saint Mark back another time under a load of pork from Alexandria."

"That was a Torcello boy."

"You're a Torcello boy."

"Yes. I'm a Basso Piave boy and a Grappa boy straight here from Pertica. I'm a Pasubio boy, too, if you know what that means. It was worse just to live there than to fight anywhere else. In the platoon they used to share anyone's gonococci brought from Schio and carried in a matchbox. They used to share this just so they could leave because it was intolerable."

"But you stayed."

"Sure," the Colonel said. "I'm always the last man to leave the party, fiesta I mean, not as in political party. The truly unpopular guest."

"Should we go?"

"I thought you had made up your mind."

"I had. But when you said it about unpopular guest it was unmade."

"Keep it made up."

"I can hold a decision."

"I know. You can hold any damn thing. But, Daughter, sometimes you don't just hold. That is for stupids. Sometimes you have to switch fast."

"I'll switch if you like."

"No. I think the decision was sound."

"But won't it be an awfully long time until morning?"

"That all depends on whether one has luck or not."

"I should sleep well."

"Yes," the Colonel said. "At your age if you can't sleep they ought to take you out and hang you."

"Oh please."

"Sorry," he said. "I meant shoot you."

"We are nearly home and you could be kind now if you wanted."

"I'm so kind I stink. Let somebody else be kind."

They were in front of the palace now and there it was; the palace. There was nothing to do now but pull the bell cord, or enter with the key. I've been lost in this place, the Colonel thought, and I was never lost in my life.

"Please kiss me good-night, kindly."

The Colonel did and loved her so he could not bear it.

She opened the door with the key, which was in her bag. Then she was gone and the Colonel was alone, with the worn pavement, the wind, which still held in the north, and the shadows from where a light went on. He walked home.

Only tourists and lovers take gondolas, he thought. Except to cross the canal in the places where there are no bridges. I ought to go to Harry's, probably, or some damn place. But I think I'll go home.

CHAPTER XV

IT WAS really home, if a hotel room can be so described. His pajamas were laid on the bed. There was a bottle of Valpolicella by the reading light, and by the bed a bottle of mineral water, in an ice bucket with a glass beside it on the silver tray. The portrait had been de-framed and was placed on two chairs where he could see it from the bed.

The Paris edition of the *New York Herald Tribune* lay on the bed beside his three pillows. He used three pillows, as Arnaldo knew, and his extra bottle of medicine, not the one that he carried in his pocket, was beside the reading light. The inner doors of the armoire, the mirrored ones, were opened in such a way, that he could see the portrait from the side. His scuffed slippers were by the bed.

I'll buy it, the Colonel said, to himself, since there was no one else there except the portrait.

He opened the Valpolicella which had been uncorked, and then re-corked, carefully, precisely, and lovingly, and poured himself a glass into the glass which was much better than any hotel should use which was faced with breakage.

"Here's to you, Daughter," he said. "You beauty and lovely. Do you know, that, among other things, you smell good always? You smell wonderfully even in a high wind or under a blanket or kissing goodnight. You know almost no one does, and you don't use scent."

She looked at him from the portrait and said nothing.

"The hell with it," he said. "I'm not going to talk to a picture."

What do you think went wrong tonight? he thought.

Me, I guess. Well I will try to be a good boy tomorrow all day; starting at first light.

"Daughter," he said, and he was talking to her, and not to a picture now. "Please know I love you and that I wish to be delicate and good. And please stay with me always now."

The picture was the same.

The Colonel took out the emeralds from his pocket, and looked at them, feeling them slide, cold and yet warm, as they take warmth, and as all good stones have warmth, from his bad hand into his good hand.

I should have put these in an envelope and locked them up, he thought. But what the effing security is there better than I can give them? I have to get these back to you fast, Daughter.

It was fun, though. And they're not worth more than a quarter of a million. What I would make in four hundred years. Have to check that figure.

He put the stones in the pocket of his pajamas and put a handkerchief over them. Then he buttoned the pocket. The first sound thing you learn, he thought, is to have flaps and buttons on all your pockets. I imagine that I learned it too early.

The stones felt good. They were hard and warm against his flat, hard, old, and warm chest, and he noted how the wind was blowing, looked at the portrait, poured another glass of Valpolicella and then started to read the Paris edition of the *New York Herald Tribune*.

I ought to take the pills, he thought. But the hell with the pills.

Then he took them just the same, and went on reading the New York Herald. He was reading Red Smith, and he liked him very much.

CHAPTER XVI

THE Colonel woke before daylight and checked that there was no one sleeping with him.

The wind was still blowing hard and he went to the open windows to check the weather. There was no light as yet in the east across the Grand Canal, but his eyes could see how rough the water was. Be a hell of a tide today, he thought. Probably flood the square. That's always fun. Except for the pigeons.

He went to the bathroom, taking the Herald Tribune and Red Smith with him, as well as a glass of Valpolicella. Damn I'll be glad when the *Gran Maestro* gets those big *fiascos*, he thought. This wine gets awfully dreggy at the end.

He sat there, with his newspaper, thinking of the things of that day.

There would be the telephone call. But it might be very late because she would be sleeping late. The young sleep late, he thought, and the beautiful sleep half again as late. She certainly would not call early, and the shops did not open until nine or a little later.

Hell, he thought, I have these damned stones. How could anyone do a thing like that?

You know how, he said to himself, reading the ads in the back of the paper. You've put it on the line enough times. It isn't crazy or morbid. She just wanted to put it on the line. It was a good thing it was me, he thought.

That is the only good thing about being me, he considered. Well I'm me, God-damn it. For better or for much worse. How would you like to sit on the can as you have sat almost every morning of your damned life with this in your pocket?

He was addressing no one, except, perhaps, posterity.

How many mornings have you sat in the row with all the others? That's the worst of it. That and shaving. Or you go off to be alone, and think or not think, and pick a good piece of cover and there are two riflemen there already, or some boy asleep.

There's no more privacy in the army than in a professional shit-house. I've never been in a professional shit-house but I imagine they run it much the same. I could learn to run one, he thought.

Then I'd make all my leading shit-house characters Ambassadors and the unsuccessful ones could be Corps-Commanders or command military districts in peace time. Don't be bitter, boy, he said to himself. It's too early in the morning and your duty's not completed yet.

What would you do with their wives, he asked himself? Buy them new hats or shoot them, he said. It's all part of the same process.

He looked at himself in the mirror, set in the half closed door. It showed him at a slight angle. It's a deflection shot, he said to himself, and they didn't lead me enough. Boy, he said, you certainly are a beat-up, old looking bastard.

Now you have to shave and look at that face while you do it. Then you must get a hair-cut. That's easy in this town. You're a Colonel of Infantry, boy. You can't go around looking like Joan of Arc or General (Brevetted) George Armstrong Custer. That beautiful horse-cavalry-man. I guess it is fun to be that way and have a loving wife and use sawdust for brains. But it must have seemed like the wrong career to him when they finished up on that hill above the Little Big Horn, with the ponies making the circle around them in all the dust, and the sage brush crushed by the hooves of the horses of the other people, and nothing left to him for the rest of his life but that old lovely black powder smell and his own people shooting each other, and themselves, because they were afraid of what the squaws would do to them.

The body was unspeakably mutilated, they used to put in this same paper. And on that hill to know you'd made one real mistake, finally, and for good, and complete with true handles. Poor horse-cavalryman, he thought. The end of all his dreams. That's one good thing about being an Infantryman. You never have any dreams except bad dreams.

Well, he said to himself, we're finished here, and pretty soon there will be good light and I can see the portrait. I'll be damned if I'll turn that in. I keep that.

Oh Christ, he said, I wonder what she looks like now sleeping. I know how she looks, he said to himself. Wonderful. She sleeps as though she had not gone to sleep. As though she were just resting. I hope she is, he thought. I hope she's resting well. Christ Jesus how I love her and I hope I never do her harm.

CHAPTER XVII

WHEN it started to be light, the Colonel saw the portrait. He, very probably, saw it as quickly as any man who was civilized and had to read and sign the forms he did not believe in, could see an object, as soon as it was visible. Yes, he said to himself, I have eyes and they have fairly fast perception still, and once they had ambition. I have led my Ruffians where they were well peppered. There are but three of the two hundred and fifty of them left alive and they are for the town's end to beg during life.

That's from Shakespeare, he told the portrait. The winner and still the undisputed champion.

Someone might take him, in a short bout. But I would rather revere him. Did you ever read King Lear, Daughter? Mister Gene Tunney did, and he was the champion of the world. But I read it too. Soldiers care for Mister Shakespeare too, though it may seem impossible. He writes like a soldier himself.

You have anything to say in your defense except to put your head back? he asked the portrait. You want some more, Shakespeare?

You don't have to defend. You just rest and leave it as it is. It's no good. Your defense and my defense is no damn good. But who could tell you to go out and hang yourself the way we do?

Nobody, he said to himself, and to the portrait. And certainly not me.

He put his good hand down and found that the room waiter had left a second bottle of Valpolicella alongside of where the first had been.

If you love a country, the Colonel thought, you might as well admit it. Sure, admit it boy.

I have loved three and lost them thrice. Give a credit. We've re-took two. Retaken, he corrected.

And we will retake the other one, General Fat Ass Franco on his shooting stick with the advice of his doctor and tame ducks and a screen of Moorish cavalry when he shoots.

Yes, he said softly to the girl who looked at him clearly now in the first and best light.

We will retake and they will all be hung upside down outside of filling stations. You have been warned, he added.

"Portrait," he said, "why the hell can't you just get into bed with me instead of being eighteen solid stone blocks away. Maybe more. I'm not as sharp now as I was; whenever."

"Portrait," he said to the girl, and to the portrait, and

to the girl both; but there wasn't any girl, and the portrait was as it was painted.

"Portrait, keep your God-damn chin up so you can break my heart easier."

It certainly was a lovely present, the Colonel thought.

"Can you maneuver?" he asked the portrait. "Good and fast?"

Portrait said nothing and the Colonel answered, You know damn well she can. She'd out-maneuver you the best day you were ever born and she would stay and fight where you would eff-off, discreetly.

"Portrait," he said. "Boy or daughter or my one true love or whatever it is; you know what it is, portrait."

The portrait, as before, did not answer. But the Colonel, who was a General now again, early in the morning at the only time he really knew, and with Valpolicella, knew as absolutely as though he had just read his third Wassermann that there was no eff-off in portrait, and he felt shame for having talked to portrait roughly.

"I'll be the best God-damned boy you ever witnessed today. And you can tell your principal that."

Portrait, as was her fashion, was silent.

She probably would speak to a horse-cavalryman, the General, for now he had two stars, and they grated on his shoulders, and showed white in the vague, scuffed red on the plaque in front of his jeep. He never used command cars, nor semi-armoured vehicles complete with sand bags.

"The hell with you, portrait," he said. "Or get your

T.S. slip from the universal chaplain of us all, with combined religions. You ought to be able to eat on that."

"The hell with you," the portrait said, without speaking. "You low class soldier."

"Yes," the Colonel said, for now he was a Colonel again, and had relinquished all his former rank.

"I love you, portrait, very much. But don't get rough with me. I love you very much because you are beautiful. But I love the girl better, a million times better, hear it?"

There was no sign that she heard it, so he tired of it.

"You are in a fixed position, portrait," he said. "Without or with any frame. And I am going to maneuver."

The portrait was as silent as she had been since the concierge had brought her into the room, and aided and abetted by the second waiter, had shown her to the Colonel and to the girl.

The Colonel looked at her and saw she was indefensible, now that the light was good, or almost good.

He saw, too, that she was the portrait of his own true love, and so he said, "I am sorry for all the stupidnesses I say. I do not wish ever to be brutal. Maybe we could both sleep a little while, with luck, and then, perhaps, your Mistress would call on the telephone?"

Maybe she will even call, he thought.

CHAPTER XVIII

THE hall porter pushed the *Gazzettino* under the door, and the Colonel had it, noiselessly, almost as soon as it had passed through the slit.

He very nearly took it from the hall porter's hand. He did not like the hall porter since he had found him, one day, going through his bag, when he, the Colonel, had re-entered the room after having left it, presumably for some time. He had to come back to the room to get his bottle of the medicine, which he had forgotten, and the hall porter was well through his bag.

"I guess you don't say stick them up in this hotel," the Colonel had said. "But you're no credit to your town."

There was silence produced, and re-produced, by the striped waist-coated man with the Fascist face, and the Colonel said, "Go on, boy, look through the rest of it. I don't carry any military secrets with my toilet articles."

Since then, there was scant friendship between them,

and the Colonel enjoyed trying to take the morning paper from the striped waist-coated man's hand; noiselessly, and when he heard, or saw it first make a move under the door.

"OK, you won today, jerk," he said in the best Venetian dialect he could summon at that hour. "Go hang yourself."

But they don't hang themselves, he thought. They just have to go on putting papers under other people's doors that do not even hate them. It must be quite a difficult trade being an ex-Fascist. Maybe he is not an ex-Fascist too. How do you know.

I can't hate Fascists, he thought. Nor Krauts either, since unfortunately, I am a soldier.

"Listen, Portrait," he said. "Do I have to hate the Krauts because we kill them? Do I have to hate them as soldiers and as human beings? It seems too easy a solution to me."

Well, portrait. Forget it. Forget it. You're not old enough to know about it. You are two years younger than the girl that you portray, and she is younger and older than hell; which is quite an old place.

"Listen, portrait," he said, and saying it, knew that now as long as he lived, he would have someone to talk to at the early hours that he woke.

"As I was saying, portrait. The hell with that too. That's too old for you too. That is one of the things you can't say no matter how true it is. There are lots of things I can never say to you and maybe that will be good for me. It is about time something was. What do you think would be good for me, Portrait?

"What's the matter, Portrait?" he asked her. "You getting hungry? I am."

So he rang the bell for the waiter who would bring breakfast.

He knew that now, even though the light was so good that every wave showed on the Grand Canal, lead colored and solid heavy with the wind, and the tide now high over the landing steps of the Palace directly opposite his room, there would be no telephone call for several hours.

The young sleep good, he thought. They deserve it.

"Why do we have to get old?" he asked the waiter who had come in with his glass-eye and the menu.

"I don't know, my Colonel. I suppose it is a natural process."

"Yes. I guess I imagine that too. The eggs fried with their faces up. Tea and toast."

"You don't want anything American?"

"The hell with anything American except me. Is the *Gran Maestro* astir yet?"

"He has your Valpolicella in the big wicker fiascos of two liters and I have brought this decanter with it."

"That one," the Colonel said. "I wish to Christ I could give him a regiment."

"I don't think he would want one, really."

"No," the Colonel said. "I don't want one, really, myself."

CHAPTER XIX

THE Colonel breakfasted with the leisure of a fighter who has been clipped badly, hears four, and knows how to relax truly for five seconds more.

"Portrait," he said. "You ought to relax too. That's the only thing that is going to be difficult about you. That's what they call the static element in painting. You know, Portrait, that almost no pictures, paintings rather, move at all. A few do. But not many.

"I wish that your mistress was here and we could have movement. How do girls like you and she know so much so damn young and be so beautiful?

"With us, if a girl is really beautiful, she comes from Texas and maybe, with luck, she can tell you what month it is. They can all count good though.

"They teach them how to count, and keep their legs together, and how to put their hair up in pin curls. Sometime, portrait, for your sins, if you have any, you ought to have to sleep in a bed with a girl who has put her hair up in pin curls to be beautiful tomorrow. Not tonight. They'd never be beautiful tonight. For tomorrow, when we make the competition.

"The girl, Renata, that you are, is sleeping now without ever having done anything to her hair. She is sleeping with it spread out on the pillow and all it is to her is a glorious, dark, silky annoyance, that she can hardly remember to comb, except that her governess taught her.

"I see her in the street with the lovely long-legged stride and the wind doing anything it wants to her hair, and her true breasts under the sweater, and then I see the nights in Texas with the pin curls; tight and subjected by metallic instruments.

"Pin me no pin curls, my beloved," he said to the Portrait, "and I will try to lay it on the line in round, heavy, hard silver dollars or with the other."

I mustn't get rough, he thought.

Then he said to the portrait, for he did not capitalize her now in his mind, "You are so God-damned beautiful you stink. Also you are jail-bait. Renata's two years older now. You are under seventeen."

And why can't I have her and love her and cherish her and never be rude, nor bad, and have the five sons that go to the five corners of the world; wherever that is? I don't know. I guess the cards we draw are those we get. You wouldn't like to re-deal would you dealer?

No. They only deal to you once, and then you pick them

up and play them. I can play them, if I draw any damn thing at all, he told portrait; who was unimpressed.

"Portrait," he said. "You better look the other way so that you will not be unmaidenly. I am going to take a shower now and shave, something you will never have to do, and put on my soldier-suit and go and walk around this town even though it is too early."

So, he got out of bed, favoring his bad leg, which hurt him always. He pulled the reading light with his bad hand. There was sufficient light, and he had been wasting electricity for nearly an hour.

He regretted this as he regretted all his errors. He walked past portrait, only looking casually, and looked at himself in the mirror. He had dropped both parts of his pajamas and he looked at himself critically and truly.

"You beat-up old bastard," he said to the mirror. Portrait was a thing of the past. Mirror was actuality and of this day.

The gut is flat, he said without uttering it. The chest is all right except where it contains the defective muscle. We are hung as we are hung, for better or worse, or something, or something awful.

You are one half a hundred years old, you bastard you. Now go in and take a shower, and scrub good, and afterwards put on your soldier suit. Today is another day.

CHAPTER XX

THE Colonel stopped at the reception desk in the lobby, but the concierge was not there yet. There was only the night porter.

"Can you put something in the safe for me?"

"No, my Colonel. No one may open the safe until the assistant manager or the concierge arrives. But I will guard anything for you that you wish."

"Thank you. It's not worth the trouble," and he buttoned the Gritti envelope, with the stones inside, the envelope addressed to himself, into the inside left pocket of his tunic.

"There's no real crime here now," the night porter said.

It had been a long night and he was happy to speak to someone. "There never really was, my Colonel. There are only differences of opinion and politics."

"What do you have for politics?" the Colonel asked; for he was lonely too.

"About what you would expect."

"I see. And how is your thing going?"

"I think it goes quite well. Maybe not as well as last year. But still quite well. We were beaten and we have to wait a while now."

"Do you work at it?"

"Not much. It is more the politics of my heart than of my head. I believe in it with my head too, but I have very little political development."

"When you get it you won't have any heart."

"Maybe not. Do you have politics in the army?"

"Plenty," the Colonel said. "But not what you mean."

"Well, we better not discuss it then. I have not meant to be intrusive."

"I asked the question; the original question rather. It was only to talk. It was not an interrogation."

"I don't think it was. You do not have the face of an inquisitor, my Colonel, and I know about the Order, although I am not a member."

"You may be member material. I'll take it up with the *Gran Maestro.*"

"We come from the same town; but from distinct quarters."

"It's a good town."

"My Colonel, I have so little political development that I believe all honorable men are honorable."

"Oh you'll get over that," the Colonel assured him. "Don't worry, boy. You've got a young party. Naturally you make errors."

"Please don't talk like that."

"It was just rough early morning joking."

"Tell me, my Colonel, what do you really think about Tito?"

"I think several things. But he's my next door neighbor. I've found it better not to talk about my neighbor."

"I'd like to learn."

"Then learn it the hard way. Don't you know people don't give answers to such questions?"

"I had hoped they did."

"They don't," the Colonel said. "Not in my position. All I can tell you is that Mister Tito has plenty problems."

"Well, I know that now truly," the night porter who was really only a boy said.

"I hope you do," the Colonel said. "I wouldn't call it, as knowledge, any pearl of great price. Now, good-day, for I must take a walk for the good of my liver, or something."

"Good day, my Colonel. *Fa brutto tempo.*"

"*Bruttissimo*," the Colonel said and, pulling the belt of his raincoat tight, and settling his shoulders into it, and the skirts well down, he stepped out into the wind.

CHAPTER XXI

THE Colonel took the ten *centesimi* gondola across the Canal, paying the usual dirty note, and standing with the crowd of those condemned to early rising.

He looked back at the Gritti and saw the windows of his room; still open. There was no promise nor threat of rain; only the same strong wild, cold wind from the mountains. Everyone in the gondola looked cold and the Colonel thought, I wish I could issue these wind-proof coats to everyone on board. God, and every officer that ever wore one, knows they are not water-proof, and who made the money out of that one?

You can't get water through a Burberry. But I suppose some able jerk has his boy in Groton now, or maybe Canterbury, where the big contractors' boys go, because our coats leaked.

And what about some brother officer of mine who split with him? I wonder who the Benny Meyers of the ground forces were? There probably wasn't only one. Probably, he thought, there must be very many. You must not be awake yet, to talk that simply. They do keep the wind out though. The raincoats. Raincoats my ass.

The gondola pulled up between the stakes on the far bank of the canal and the Colonel watched the black-clad people climb up out of the black-painted vehicle. Is she a vehicle? he thought. Or must a vehicle have wheels or be tracked?

Nobody would give you a penny for your thoughts, he thought. Not this morning. But I've seen them worth a certain amount of money when the chips were down.

He penetrated into the far side of the city, the side that finally fronted on the Adriatic, and that he liked the best. He was going in by a very narrow street, and he was going to not keep track of the number of more or less north and south streets that he crossed, nor count the bridges, and then try and orient himself so he would come out at the market without getting up any dead ends.

It was a game you play, as some people used to play double Canfield or any solitary card games. But it had the advantage of you moving while you do it and that you look at the houses, the minor vistas, the shops and the *trattorias* and at old palaces of the city of Venice while you are walking. If you loved the city of Venice it was an excellent game.

It is a sort of *solitaire ambulante* and what you win is the happiness of your eye and heart. If you made the market, on this side of town, without ever being stymied, you won the game. But you must not make it too easy and you must not count.

On the other side of the town, game was to leave from the Gritti and make the Rialto by the *Fondamente Nuove* without a mistake.

Then you could climb the bridge and cross it and go down into the market. He liked the market best. It was the part of any town he always went to first.

Just then he heard the two young men behind him saying the things about him. He knew they were young men by their voices and he did not look back, but listened carefully for distance and waited for the next turn to see them, as he turned.

They are on their way to work, he decided. Maybe they are former Fascists or maybe they are something else, or maybe it is just the line that they are talking. But they are making it pretty personal now. It isn't just Americans, it is also me, myself, my gray hair, the slightly crooked way I walk, the combat boots (those, of that stripe, disliked the practicability of combat boots. They liked boots that rang on the flag stones and took a high black polish.).

It is my uniform which they find to be without grace. Now it is why I am walking at this hour, and now it is their absolute security that I can no longer make love.

The Colonel swung sharp to the left at the next corner, seeing what he had to deal with and the exact distance, and when the two young men came around the corner which was formed by the apse of the church of Frari there was no Colonel. He was in the dead angle behind the apse of the ancient church and as they passed, he, hearing them come by their talk, stepped out with a hand in each low pocket of his raincoat and turned himself, and the raincoat, with the two hands in the pockets, toward them.

They stopped and he looked at them both in the face and smiled his old and worn death smile. Then he looked down at their feet, as you always look at the feet of such people, since they wear their shoes too tight, and when you take the shoes off them you see their hammer-toes. The Colonel spat on the pavement and said nothing.

The two of them, they *were* the first thing he had suspected, looked at him with hatred and with that other thing. Then they were off like marsh-birds, walking with the long strides of herons too, the Colonel thought, and something of the flight of curlews, and looking back with hatred, waiting to have the last word if the distance was ever safe.

It is a pity they weren't ten against one, the Colonel thought. They might have fought. I should not blame them, since they were defeated.

But their manners were not good in respect to a man of my rank and age. Also it was not intelligent to think all fifty year old Colonels would not understand their language. Nor was it intelligent to think old Infantrymen would not fight this early in the morning against the simple odds of two to one.

I'd hate to fight in this town where I love the people. I would avoid it. But couldn't those badly educated youths realize what sort of animal they were dealing with? Don't they know how you get to walk that way? Nor any of the other signs that combat people show as surely as a fisherman's hands tell you if he is a fisherman from the creases from the cord cuts.

It is true they only saw my back and ass and legs and boots. But you'd think they might have told from the way they must move. Maybe they don't anymore. But when I had a chance to look at them and think, Take the two of them out and hang them, I believe they understood. They understood quite clearly.

What's a man life worth anyway? Ten thousand dollars if his insurance is paid up in our army. What the hell has that got to do with it. Oh yes, that was what I was thinking about before those jerks showed; how much money I had saved my government, in my time when people like Benny Meyers were in the trough.

Yes, he said, and how much you lost them at the Chateau that time at ten G's a head. Well nobody ever really understood it except me, I guess. There's no reason to tell them now. Your commanding general sometimes puts things down as the Fortunes of War. Back at Army they know such things are bound to happen. You do it, as ordered, with a big butcher-bill and you're a hero.

Christ, I am opposed to the excessive butcher-bill, he thought. But you get the orders, and you have to carry them out. It is the mistakes that are no good to sleep with. But why the hell sleep with them anyway. It never did any good. But they can certainly crawl into a sack sometimes. They can crawl in and stay in there with you.

Cheer up, boy, he said. Remember you had a lot of money on you when you picked that one. And you might have been stripped if you lost. You can't fight a lick anymore with your hands, and you didn't have any weapon.

So don't be gloomy, boy, or man, or Colonel, or busted General. We're almost to the market now and you made it without hardly noticing.

Hardly noticing is bad, he added.

CHAPTER XXII

HE loved the market. A great part of it was close-packed and crowded into several side streets, and it was so concentrated that it was difficult not to jostle people, unintentionally, and each time you stopped to look, to buy, or to admire, you formed an *îlot de résistance* against the flow of the morning attack of the purchasers.

The Colonel liked to study the spread and high piled cheeses and the great sausages. People at home think *mortadella* is a sausage, he thought.

Then he said to the woman in the booth, "Let me try a little of that sausage, please. Only a sliver."

She cut a thin, paper thin, slice for him, ferociously, and lovingly, and when the Colonel tasted it, there was the half smokey, black pepper-corned, true flavor of the meat from the hogs that ate acorns in the mountains.

"I will take a quarter of a kilo."

The Barone's lunches for the shooting blinds were of a

Spartan quality, which the Colonel respected, since he knew no one should eat much while shooting. He felt, though, that he might augment the lunch with this sausage, and share it with the poler and picker-upper. He might give a slice to Bobby, the retriever, who would be wet through to his hide many times, and enthusiastic still, but shaking with cold.

"Is this the best sausage that you have?" he asked the woman. "Have you nothing that does not show and is reserved for better and steadier customers?"

"This is the best sausage. There are many other sausages, as you know. But this is the best."

"Then give me one eighth of a kilo of a sausage that is highly fortifying, but is not highly seasoned."

"I have it," she said. "It is a little new but exactly as you describe."

This sausage was for Bobby.

But you do not say that you buy sausages for a dog in Italy where the worst crime is to be considered a fool and many people go hungry. You may give expensive sausage to a dog before a man who works for his living and knows what a dog goes through in water in cold weather. But you do not buy them, stating your purpose in possessing them, unless you are a fool, or a millionaire from the war and from after.

The Colonel paid for the wrapped-up package and proceeded on through the market inhaling the smell of roasted coffee and looking at the amount of fat on each carcass in the butcher section, as though he were enjoying the Dutch painters, whose names no one remembers, who painted, in perfection of detail, all things you shot, or that were eatable.

A market is the closest thing to a good museum like the Prado or as the Accademia is now, the Colonel thought.

He took a short cut, and was at the fish-market.

In the market, spread on the slippery stone floor, or in their baskets, or their rope-handled boxes, were the heavy, gray-green lobsters with their magenta overtones that presaged their death in boiling water. They have all been captured by treachery, the Colonel thought, and their claws are pegged.

There were the small soles, and there were a few albacore and bonito. These last, the Colonel thought, looked like boat-tailed bullets, dignified in death, and with the huge eye of the pelagic fish.

They were not made to be caught except for their voraciousness. The poor sole exists, in shallow water, to feed man. But these other roving bullets, in their great bands, live in blue water and travel through all oceans and all seas.

A nickel for your thoughts now, he thought. Let's see what else they have.

There were many eels, alive and no longer confident in their eeldom. There were fine prawns that could make a *scampi brochetto* spitted and broiled on a rapier-like instrument that could be used as a Brooklyn icepick. There were medium sized shrimp, gray and opalescent, awaiting their turn, too, for the boiling water and their immortality, to

have their shucked carcasses float out easily on an ebb tide
on the Grand Canal.

The speedy shrimp, the Colonel thought, with tentacles
longer than the mustaches of that old Japanese admiral,
comes here now to die for our benefit. Oh Christian shrimp,
he thought, master of retreat, and with your wonderful
intelligence service in those two light whips, why did they
not teach you about nets and that lights are dangerous?

Must have been some slip-up, he thought.

Now he looked at the many small crustaceans, the razor-
edge clams you only should eat raw if you had your
typhoid shots up to date, and all the small delectables.

He went past these, stopping to ask one seller where
his clams came from. They came from a good place, without sewerage and the Colonel asked to have six opened. He
drank the juice and cut the clam out, cutting close against
the shell with the curved knife the man handed him. The
man had handed him the knife because he knew from
experience the Colonel cut closer to the shell than he had
been taught to cut.

The Colonel paid him the pittance that they cost, which
must have been much greater than the pittance those received who caught them, and he thought, now I must see
the stream and canal fishes and get back to the hotel.

CHAPTER XXIII

THE Colonel arrived at the lobby of the Hotel Gritti-Palace. His gondolieres were paid off and, now, inside the hotel, there was no wind.

It had taken two men to bring the gondola up the Grand Canal from the market. They had both worked hard, and he had paid them what it was worth, and some more.

"Are there any calls for me?" he asked the concierge, who was now in attendance.

The concierge was light, fast, sharp-faced, intelligent and polite, always, without subservience. He wore the crossed keys of his office on the lapels of his blue uniform without ostentation. He was the concierge. It is a rank very close to that of Captain, the Colonel thought. An officer and not a Gentleman. Make it top sergeant in the old days; except he's dealing always with the brass.

"My lady has called twice," the concierge said in English. Or whatever that language should be called we all speak, the Colonel thought. Leave it at English. That is about what they have left. They should be allowed to keep the name of the language. Cripps will probably ration it shortly anyway.

"Please put me through to her at once," he told the concierge.

The concierge commenced to dial numbers.

"You may talk over there, my Colonel," he said. "I have made the connection."

"You're fast."

"Over there," the concierge said.

Inside the booth the Colonel lifted the receiver and said, automatically, "Colonel Cantwell speaking."

"I called twice, Richard," the girl said. "But they explained that you were out. Where were you?"

"At the market. How are you, my lovely?"

"No one listens on this phone at this hour. I am your lovely. Whoever that is."

"You. Did you sleep well?"

"It was like ski-ing in the dark. Not really ski-ing but really dark."

"That's the way it should be. Why did you wake so early? You've frightened my concierge."

"If it is not un-maidenly, how soon can we meet, and where?"

"Where you wish and when you wish."

"Do you still have the stones and did Miss Portrait help any?"

"Yes to both questions. The stones are in my upper left

hand pocket buttoned down. Miss Portrait and I talked late and early and it made everything much easier."

"Do you love her more than me?"

"I'm not abnormal yet. Perhaps that's bragging. But she's lovely."

"Where should we meet?"

"Should we have breakfast at the Florian, on the right hand side of the square? The square should be flooded and it will be fun to watch."

"I'll be there in twenty minutes if you want me."

"I want you," the Colonel said and hung up.

Coming out of the telephone booth he, suddenly, did not feel good and then he felt as though the devil had him in an iron cage, built like an iron lung or an iron maiden, and he walked, gray-faced, to the concierge's desk and said, in Italian, "Domenico, Ico, could you get me a glass of water, please?"

The concierge was gone and he leaned on the desk resting. He rested lightly and without illusion. Then the concierge was back with the glass of water, and he took four tablets of the type that you take two, and he continued resting as lightly as a hawk rests.

"Domenico," he said.

"Yes."

"I have something here in an envelope that you can put in the safe. It may be called for either by myself, in person, or in writing, or by the person you have just put that call through to. Would you like that in writing?"

"No. It would be unnecessary."

196

"But what about you, boy? You're not immortal, are you?"

"Fairly so," the concierge told him. "But I will put it in writing, and after me, comes the Manager and the Assistant Manager."

"Both good men," the Colonel agreed.

"Wouldn't you like to sit down, my Colonel?"

"No. Who sits down except men and women in change of life hotels? Do you sit down?"

"No."

"I can rest on my feet, or against a God damned tree. My countrymen sit down, or lie down, or fall down. Give them a few energy crackers to stall their whimpers."

He was talking too much to regain confidence quickly.

"Do they really have energy crackers?"

"Sure. It has something in it that keeps you from getting erections. It's like the atomic bomb, only played backwards."

"I can't believe it."

"We have the most terrific military secrets that one General's wife ever told another. Energy crackers is the least of it. Next time we will give all Venice botulism from 56,000 feet. There's nothing to it," the Colonel explained. "They give you anthrax, and you give them botulism."

"But it will be horrible."

"It will be worse than that," the Colonel assured him. "This isn't classified. It's all been published. And while it goes on you can hear Margaret, if you tune in right, singing the Star Spangled Banner on the radio. I think that could be arranged. The voice I would not describe as a big one. Not as we know voices who have heard the good ones in our time. But everything is a trick now. The radio can almost make the voice. And the Star Spangled Banner is fool-proof until toward the last."

"Do you think they will drop anything here?"

"No. They never have."

The Colonel, who was four star general now, in his wrath and in his agony and in his need for confidence, but secured temporarily through the absorption of the tablets, said, "*Ciao*, Domenico," and left the Gritti.

He figured it took twelve and one half minutes to reach the place where his true love would probably arrive a little late. He walked it carefully and at the speed he should walk it. The bridges were all the same.

CHAPTER XXIV

HIS true love was at the table at the exact time that she said she would be· She was as beautiful as always in the hard, morning light that came across the flooded square, and she said. 'Please, Richard. Are you all right? Please?"

"Sure," the Colonel said. "You wonder beauty."

"Did you go to all our places in the market?"

"Only a few of them. I did not go to where they have the wild ducks."

"Thank you."

"For nothing," the Colonel said. "I never go there when we are not together."

"Don't you think I should go to the shoot?"

"No. I am quite sure. Alvarito would have asked you if he wanted you."

"He might not have asked me because he wanted me."

"That's true," the Colonel said, and pondered that for two seconds. "What do you want for breakfast?"

"Breakfast is worthless here, and I don't like the square when it is flooded. It is sad and the pigeons have no place to alight. It is only really fun toward the last when the children play. Should we go and have breakfast at the Gritti?"

"Do you want to?"

"Yes."

"Good. We'll have breakfast there. I've had mine already."

"Really?"

"I'll have some coffee and hot rolls, and only feel them with my fingers. Are you awfully hungry?"

"Awfully," she said, truly.

"We'll give breakfast the full treatment," the Colonel said. "You'll wish you had never heard of breakfast."

As they walked, with the wind at their back, and her hair blowing better than any banner, she asked him, holding close, "Do you still love me in the cold, hard Venice light of morning? It is really cold and hard isn't it?"

"I love you and it is cold and hard."

"I loved you all night when I was ski-ing in the dark."

"How do you do that?"

"It is the same runs except that it is dark and the snow is dark instead of light. You ski the same; controlled and good."

"Did you ski all night? That would be many runs."

"No. Afterwards I slept soundly and well and I woke happy. You were with me and you were asleep like a baby."

"I wasn't with you and I was not asleep."

"You're with me now," she said and held close and tight.

"And we are almost there."

"Yes."

"Have I told you, yet, properly, that I love you?"

"You told me. But tell me again."

"I love you," he said. "Take it frontally and formally please."

"I take it anyway you want as long as it is true."

"That's the proper attitude," he said. "You good, brave, lovely girl. Turn your hair sideways once on top of this bridge and let it blow obliquely."

He had made a concession, with obliquely, instead of saying, correctly, oblique.

"That's easy," she said. "Do you like it?"

He looked and saw the profile and the wonder early morning colour and her chest upstanding in the black sweater and her eyes in the wind and he said, "Yes. I like it."

"I'm very glad," she said.

CHAPTER XXV

A T the Gritti, the *Gran Maestro* seated them at the table which was beside the window that looked out on the Grand Canal. There was no one else in the dining room.

The *Gran Maestro* was festive and well with the morning. He took his ulcers day by day, and his heart the same way. When they did not hurt he did not hurt either.

"Your pitted compatriot eats in bed at his hotel, my colleague tells me," he confided to the Colonel. "We may have a few Belgians. 'The bravest of these were the Belgians,' " he quoted. "There is a pair of *pescecani* from you know where. But they are exhausted and I believe they will eat, as pigs, in their room."

"An excellent situation report," the Colonel said. "Our problem, *Gran Maestro*, is that I have already eaten in my room as pitted does and as the *pescecani* will. But this lady—"

"Young girl," interrupted the *Gran Maestro* with his

whole-face smile. He was feeling very good since it was a completely new day.

"This very young lady wants a breakfast to end breakfasts."

"I understand," the *Gran Maestro* said and he looked at Renata and his heart rolled over as a porpoise does in the sea. It is a beautiful movement and only a few people in this world can feel it and accomplish it.

"What do you want to eat, Daughter?" the Colonel asked, looking at her early morning, unretouched dark beauty.

"Everything."

"Would you give any suggestions?"

"Tea instead of coffee and whatever the *Gran Maestro* can salvage."

"It won't be salvage, Daughter," said the *Gran Maestro*.

"I'm the one who calls her Daughter."

"I said it honestly," the *Gran Maestro* said. "We can make or *fabricar rognons* grilled with champignons dug by people I know. Or, raised in damp cellars. There can be an omelet with truffles dug by pigs of distinction. There can be real Canadian bacon from maybe Canada, even."

"Wherever that is," the girl said happily and unillusioned.

"Wherever that is," said the Colonel seriously. "And I know damn well where it is."

"I think we should stop the jokes now and get to the breakfast."

"If it is not unmaidenly I think so too. Mine is a decanted flask of the Valpolicella."

"Nothing else?"

"Bring me one ration of the alleged Canadian bacon," the Colonel said.

He looked at the girl, since they were alone now, and he said, "How are you my dearest?"

"Quite hungry, I suppose. But thank you for being good for so long a time."

"It was easy," the Colonel told her in Italian.

CHAPTER XXVI

THEY sat there at the table and watched the early stormy light over the Canal. The grey had turned to a yellow grey, now, with the sun, and the waves were working against the outgoing tide.

"Mummy says she can't live here too long at any time because there are no trees," the girl said. "That's why she goes to the country."

"That's why everyone goes to the country," the Colonel said. "We could plant a few trees if we found a place with a big enough garden."

"I like Lombardy poplars and plane trees the best, but I am still quite uneducated."

"I like them, and cypresses and chestnut trees. The real chestnut and the horse-chestnut. But you will never see trees, Daughter, until we go to America. Wait till you see a white pine or a ponderosa pine."

"Will we see them when we make the long trip and

stop at all the filling stations or comfort stations or whatever they are called?"

"Lodges and Tourist Camps," the Colonel said. "Those others we stop at; but not for the night."

"I want so much for us to roll up to a comfort station and plank down my money and tell them to fill her up and check the oil, Mac, the way it is in American books or in the films."

"That's a filling station."

"Then what is a comfort station?"

"Where you go, you know—"

"Oh," the girl said and blushed. "I'm sorry. I want to learn American so much. But I suppose I shall say barbarous things the way you do sometimes in Italian."

"It is an easy language. The further West you go the straighter and the easier it becomes."

The *Gran Maestro* brought the breakfast and the odor of it, although it did not spread through the room, due to the silver covers on the dishes, came to them steady and as broiled bacon and kidneys, with the dark lusterless smell of grilled mushrooms added.

"It looks lovely," the girl said. "Thank you very much, *Gran Maestro*. Should I talk American?" she asked the Colonel. She extended her hand to the *Gran Maestro* lightly, and fastly, so that it darted as a rapier does, and said, "Put it there, Pal. This grub is tops."

The *Gran Maestro* said, "Thank you, my lady."

"Should I have said chow instead of grub?" the girl asked the Colonel.

"They are really interchangeable."

"Did they talk like that out West when you were a boy? What would you say at breakfast?"

"Breakfast was served, or offered up, by the cook. He would say, 'Come and get it, you sons of bitches, or I'll throw it away.'"

"I must learn that for in the country. Sometimes when we have the British Ambassador and his dull wife for dinner I will teach the footman, who will announce dinner, to say, 'Come and get it, you son of bitches, or we will throw it away.'"

"He'd devaluate," the Colonel said. "At any rate, it would be an interesting experiment."

"Tell me something I can say in true American to the pitted one if he comes in. I will just whisper it in his ear as though I were making a rendezvous, as they did in the old days."

"It would depend on how he looks. If he is very dejected looking, you might whisper to him, 'Listen, Mac. You hired out to be tough, didn't you?'"

"That's lovely," she said and repeated it in a voice she had learned from Ida Lupino. "Can I say it to the *Gran Maestro*?"

"Sure. Why not. *Gran Maestro!*"

The *Gran Maestro* came over and leaned forward attentively.

"Listen, Mac. You hired out to be tough, didn't you?" the girl hard-worded him.

"I did indeed," the *Gran Maestro* said. "Thank you for stating it so exactly."

"If that one comes in and you wish to speak to him

after he has eaten, just whisper in his ear, 'Wipe the egg off your chin, Jack, and straighten up and fly right.' "

"I'll remember it and I'll practice it at home."

"What are we going to do after breakfast?"

"Should we go up and look at the picture and see if it is of any value, I mean any good, in daylight?"

"Yes," the Colonel said.

CHAPTER XXVII

UPSTAIRS the room was already done and the Colonel, who had anticipated a possible messiness of locale, was pleased.

"Stand by it once," he said. Then remembered to add, "Please."

She stood by it, and he looked at it from where he had looked at it last night.

"There's no comparison, of course," he said. "I don't mean likeness. The likeness is excellent."

"Was there supposed to be a comparison?" the girl asked, and swung her head back and stood there with the black sweater of the portrait.

"Of course not. But last night, and at first light, I talked to the portrait as though it were you."

"That was nice of you and shows it has served some useful purpose."

They were lying now on the bed and the girl said to him, "Don't you ever close windows?"

"No. Do you?"

"Only when it rains."

"How much alike are we?"

"I don't know. We never had much of a chance to find out."

"We've never had a fair chance. But we've had enough of a chance for me to know."

"And when you know what the hell have you got?" the Colonel asked.

"I don't know. Something better than there is, I suppose."

"Sure. We ought to try for that. I don't believe in limited objectives. Sometimes you're forced to, though."

"What is your great sorrow?"

"Other people's orders," he said. "What's yours?"

"You."

"I don't want to be a sorrow. I've been a sorry son of a bitch many times. But I never was anybody's sorrow."

"Well you are mine now."

"All right," he said. "We'll take it that way."

"You're nice to take it that way. You're very kind this morning. I'm so ashamed about how things are. Please hold me very close and let's not talk, or think, about how things might have been different."

"Daughter, that's one of the few things I know how to do."

"You know many, many things. Don't say such a thing."

"Sure," the Colonel said. "I know how to fight forwards and how to fight backwards and what else?"

"About pictures and about books and about life."

"That's easy. You just look at the pictures without prejudice, and you read the books with as open a mind as you have, and you live life."

"Don't take off your tunic, please."

"All right."

"You do anything when I say please."

"I have done things without."

"Not very often."

"No," the Colonel agreed. "Please is a pretty word."

"Please, please, please."

"*Per piacere*. It means for pleasure. I wish we always talked Italian."

"We could in the dark. Although there are things that say better in English.

"I love you my last true and only love," she quoted. "When lilacs last in the door-yard bloomed. And out of the cradle endlessly rocking. And come and get it, you sons of bitches, or I'll throw it away. You don't want those in other languages do you, Richard?"

"No."

"Kiss me again, please."

"Unnecessary please."

"I would probably end up as an unnecessary please myself. That is the good thing about you going to die that you can't leave me."

"That's a little rough," the Colonel said. "Watch your beautiful mouth a little on that."

"I get rough when you get rough," she said. "You wouldn't want me to be completely otherwise?"

"I would not want you to be in any way other than you are and I love you truly, finally and for good."

"You say nice things very clearly sometimes. What was it happened with you and your wife, if I may ask?"

"She was an ambitious woman and I was away too much."

"You mean she went away, from ambition, when you only were away from duty?"

"Sure," the Colonel said and remembered, as unbitterly as he could. "She had more ambition than Napoleon and about the talent of the average High School Valedictorian."

"Whatever that is," the girl said. "But let's not speak about her. I'm sorry I asked the question. She must be sad that she is not with you."

"No. She is too conceited ever to be sad, and she married me to advance herself in Army circles, and have better contacts for what she considered her profession, or her art. She was a journalist."

"But they are dreadful," the girl said.

"I agree."

"But you couldn't have married a woman journalist that kept on being that?"

"I told you I made mistakes," the Colonel said.

"Let's talk about something nice."

"Let's."

"But that was terrible. How could you have done such a thing?"

"I don't know. I could tell you in detail but let's skip it."

"Please let's skip it. But I had no idea it was something as awful as that. You wouldn't do such a thing now, would you?"

"I promise you, my sweet."

"But you don't ever write to her?"

"Of course not."

"You wouldn't tell her about us, so she could write about it?"

"No. I told her about things once, and she wrote about them. But that was in another country and besides the wench is dead."

"Is she really dead?"

"Deader than Phoebus the Phoenician. But she doesn't know it yet."

"What would you do if we were together in the Piazza and you saw her?"

"I'd look straight through her to show her how dead she was."

"Thank you very much," the girl said. "You know that another woman, or a woman in memory, is a terrible thing for a young girl to deal with when she is still without experience."

"There isn't any other woman," the Colonel told her, and his eyes were bad and remembering. "Nor is there any woman of memory."

"Thank you very much," the girl said. "When I look at you I believe it truly. But please never look at me nor think of me like that."

"Should we hunt her down and hang her to a high tree?" the Colonel said with anticipation.

"No. Let us forget her."

"She is forgotten," the Colonel said. And, strangely enough, she was. It was strange because she had been present in the room for a moment, and she had very nearly caused a panic; which is one of the strangest things there is, the Colonel thought. He knew about panics.

But she was gone now, for good and forever; cauterized; exorcised and with the eleven copies of her reclassification papers, in which was included the formal, notarized act of divorcement, in triplicate.

"She is forgotten," the Colonel said. It was quite true.

"I'm so pleased," the girl said. "I don't know why they ever let her into the hotel."

"We're enough alike," the Colonel said. "We better not carry it too God damned far."

"You can hang her if you wish because she is why we cannot marry."

"She's forgotten," the Colonel told her. "Maybe she will take a good look at herself in the mirror sometime and hang herself."

"Now that she is out of the room we should wish her no bad luck. But, as a good Venetian, I wish that she were dead."

"So do I," the Colonel said. "And now, since she is not, let us forget her for keeps."

"For keeps and for always," the girl said. "I hope that is the correct diction. Or in Spanish *para sempre*."

"Para sempre and his brother," the Colonel said·

CHAPTER XXVIII

THEY lay together now and did not speak and the Colonel felt her heart beat. It is easy to feel a heart beat under a black sweater knitted by someone in the family, and her dark hair lay, long and heavy, over his good arm. It isn't heavy, he thought, it is lighter than anything there is. She lay, quiet and loving, and whatever it was that they possessed was in complete communication. He kissed her on the mouth, gently and hungrily, and then it was as though there was static, suddenly, when communications had been perfect.

"Richard," she said. "I'm sorry about things."

"Never be sorry," the Colonel said. "Never discuss casualties, Daughter."

"Say it again."

"Daughter."

"Will you tell me some happy things I can have for during the week and some more of war for my education?"

"Let's skip war."

"No. I need it for my education."

"I do too," the Colonel said. "Not maneuvers. You know, in our army once, a general officer through chicanery obtained the plan of the maneuver. He anticipated every move of the enemy force and comported himself so brilliantly that he was promoted over many better men. And that was why we got smacked one time. That and the prevalence of week-ends."

"We're on a week-end now."

"I know," the Colonel said. "I can still count up to seven."

"But are you bitter about everything?"

"No. It is just that I am half a hundred years old and I know things."

"Tell me something more about Paris because I love to think of you and Paris in the week."

"Daughter, why don't you lay off Paris?"

"But I've been in Paris, and I will go back there again, and I want to know. It is the loveliest city in the world, next to our own, and I want to know some things truly to take with me."

"We will go together and I will tell you there."

"Thank you. But tell me a little now for this week only."

"Leclerc was a high-born jerk as I think that I've explained. Very brave, very arrogant, and extremely ambitious. He is dead, as I said."

"Yes, you told me."

"They say you should never speak ill of the dead. But I

think it is the best time to speak truly of them. I have never said anything of a dead that I would not say to his face," and he added, "in spades."

"Let's not talk about him. I have reclassified him in my mind."

"What do you want then; picturesque?"

"Yes please. I have bad taste from reading the illustrated papers. But I will read Dante all week while you are gone. I'll go to mass each morning. That should be enough."

"Go to Harry's before lunch too."

"I will," she said. "Please tell me some picturesque."

"Don't you think we might better just go to sleep?"

"How can we go to sleep now when we have so little time? Feel this," she said and pushed her whole head up under his chin until she forced his head back.

"All right, I'll talk."

"Give me your hand first to hold. I'll have it in my hand when I read the Dante and do the other things."

"Dante was an execrable character. More conceited than Leclerc."

"I know. But he did not write execrably."

"No. Leclerc could fight too. Excellently."

"Now tell me."

Her head was on his chest now, and the Colonel said, "Why did you not want me to take off the tunic?"

"I like to feel the buttons. Is it wrong?"

"I'll be a sad son of a bitch," the Colonel said. "How many people fought in your family?"

"Everybody," she said. "Always. They were traders as well and several of them were Doges of this city as you know."

"But they all fought?"

"All," she said. "As far as I know."

"OK," the Colonel said. "I'll tell you any God damn thing you want to know."

"Just something picturesque. As bad or worse than in the illustrated papers."

"*Domenica del Corriere* or *Tribuna Illustrata?*"

"Worse if possible."

"Kiss me first."

She kissed him kind, and hard, and desperately, and the Colonel could not think about any fights or any picturesque or strange incidents. He only thought of her and how she felt and how close life comes to death when there is ecstasy. And what the hell is ecstasy and what's ecstasy's rank and serial number? And how does her black sweater feel. And who made all her smoothness and delight and the strange pride and sacrifice and wisdom of a child? Yes, ecstasy is what you might have had and instead you draw sleep's other brother.

Death is a lot of shit, he thought. It comes to you in small fragments that hardly show where it has entered. It comes, sometimes, atrociously. It can come from unboiled water; an un-pulled-up mosquito boot, or it can come with the great, white-hot, clanging roar we have lived with. It comes in small cracking whispers that precede the noise of the automatic weapon. It can come with the smoke-emitting arc of the grenade, or the sharp, cracking drop of the mortar.

I have seen it come, loosening itself from the bomb rack, and falling with that strange curve. It comes in the metallic rending crash of a vehicle, or the simple lack of traction on a slippery road.

It comes in bed to most people, I know, like love's opposite number. I have lived with it nearly all my life and the dispensing of it has been my trade. But what can I tell this girl now on this cold, windy morning in the Gritti Palace Hotel?

"What would you like to know, Daughter?" he asked her.

"Everything."

"All right," the Colonel said. "Here goes."

CHAPTER XXIX

THEY lay on the pleasantly hard, new-made bed with their legs pressed tight against one another, and her head was on his chest, and her hair spread across his old hard neck; and he told her.

"We landed without much opposition. They had the true opposition at the other beach. Then we had to link up with the people who had been dropped, and take and secure various towns, and then we took Cherbourg. This was difficult, and had to be done very fast, and the orders were from a General called Lightning Joe that you never would have heard of. Good General."

"Go on, please. You spoke about Lightning Joe before."

"After Cherbourg we had everything. I took nothing but an Admiral's compass because I had a small boat at that time on Chesapeake Bay. But we had all the Wehrmacht stamped Martell and some people had as much as six million

German printed French francs. They were good until a year ago, and at that time they were worth fifty to the dollar, and many a man has a tractor now instead of simply one mule who knew how to send them home through his Esses, or sometimes his G's.

"I never stole anything except the compass because I thought it was bad luck to steal, unnecessarily, in war. But I drank the cognac and I used to try to figure out the different corrections on the compass when I had time. The compass was the only friend I had, and the telephone was my life. We had more wire strung than there are cunts in Texas."

"Please keep telling me and be as little rough as you can. I don't know what the word means and I don't want to know."

"Texas is a big state," the Colonel said. "That is why I used it and its female population as a symbol. You cannot say more cunts than Wyoming because there are less than thirty thousand there, perhaps, hell, make it fifty, and there was a lot of wire, and you kept stringing it and rolling it up, and stringing it again."

"Go on."

"We will cut to the break-through," the Colonel said. "Please tell me if this bores you."

"No."

"So we made the mucking break-through," the Colonel said, and now his head was turned to her head, and he was not lecturing; he was confessing.

"The first day most of them came over and dropped the

Christmas tree ornaments that confuse the other people's radar and it was called off. We were ready to go but they called it off. Quite properly I am sure. I love **the very** highest brass like I love the pig's you know."

"Tell it to me and don't be bad."

"Conditions were not propitious," the Colonel said. "So the second day we were for it, as our British cousins, who could not fight their way out of a wet tissue towel, say, and over came the people of the wild, blue yonder.

"They were still taking off from the fields where they lived on that green-grassed aircraft carrier that they called England, when we saw the first of them.

"Shining, bright and beautiful, because they had scraped the invasion paint by then, or maybe they had not. My memory is not exact about this part.

"Anyway, Daughter, you could see the line of them going back toward the east further than you could see. It was like a great train. They were high in the sky and never more beautiful. I told my S-2 that we should call them the Valhalla Express. Are you tired of it?"

"No. I can see the Valhalla Express. We never saw it in such numbers. But we saw it. Many times."

"We were back two thousand yards from where we were to take off from. You know what two thousand yards is, Daughter, in a war when you are attacking?"

"No. How could I?"

"Then the front part of the Valhalla Express dropped coloured smoke and turned and went home. This smoke was dropped accurately, and clearly showed the target which was the Kraut positions. They were good positions and it *might* have been impossible to move him out of them without something mighty and picturesque such as we were experiencing.

"Then, Daughter, the next sections of the Valhalla express dropped everything in the world on the Krauts and where they lived and worked to hold us up. Later it looked as though all of the earth had erupted and the prisoners that we took shook as a man shakes when his malaria hits him. They were very brave boys from the Sixth Parachute Division and they all shook and could not control it though they tried.

"So you can see it was a good bombing. Just the thing we always need in this life. Make them tremble in the fear of justice and of might.

"So then daughter, not to bore you, the wind was from the east and the smoke began to blow back in our direction. The heavies were bombing on the smoke line and the smoke line was now over us. Therefore they bombed us the same as they had bombed the Krauts. First it was the heavies, and no one need ever worry about hell who was there that day. Then, to really make the break-through good and to leave as few people as possible on either side, the mediums came over and bombed who was left. Then we made the break-through as soon as the Valhalla Express had gone home, stretching in its beauty and its majesty from that part of France to all over England."

If a man has a conscience, the Colonel thought, he might think about air-power some time.

"Give me a glass of that Valpolicella," the Colonel said, and remembered to add, "please."

"Excuse me," he said. "Be comfortable, honey dog, please. You asked me to tell you."

"I'm not your honey dog. That must be someone else."

"Correct. You're my last and true and only love. Is that correct? But you asked me to tell you."

"Please tell me," the girl said. "I'd like to be your honey dog if I knew how to do it. But I am only a girl from this town that loves you."

"We'll operate on that," the Colonel said. "And I love you. I probably picked up that phrase in the Philippines."

"Probably," the girl said. "But I would rather be your straight girl."

"You are," the Colonel said. "Complete with handles and with the flag on top."

"Please don't be rough," she said. "Please love me true and tell me as true as you can, without hurting yourself in any way."

"I'll tell you true," he said. "As true as I can tell and let it hurt who it hurts. It is better that you hear it from me, if you have curiosity on this subject, than that you read it in some book with stiff covers."

"Please don't be rough. Just tell me true and hold me tight and tell me true until you are purged of it; if that can be."

"I don't need to purge," he said. "Except heavies being used tactically. I have nothing against them if they use them right even if they kill you. But for ground support give me a man like Pete Quesada. There is a man who will boot them in."

"Please."

"If you ever want to quit a beat-up character like me that guy could give you ground support."

"You are not beat-up, whatever that is, and I love you."

"Please give me two tablets from that bottle and pour the glass of Valpolicella that you neglected to pour, and I will tell you some of the rest of it."

"You don't have to. You don't have to tell me and I know now it is not good for you. Especially not the Valhalla Express day. I am not an inquisitor; or whatever the female of inquisitor is. Let us just lie quietly and look out of the window, and watch and see what happens on our Grand Canal."

"Maybe we better. Who gives a damn about the war anyway?"

"You and me, maybe," she said and stroked his head. "Here are the two things from the square bottle. Here is the glass of decanted vino. I'll send you better from our own estates. Please let us sleep a little while. Please be a good boy and we just lie together and love each other. Please put your hand here."

"My good or my bad?"

"Your bad," the girl said. "The one I love and must think about all week. I cannot keep it like you keep the stones."

"They're in the safe," the Colonel said. "In your name," he added.

"Let's just sleep and not talk about any material things nor any sorrows."

"The hell with sorrows," the Colonel said with his eyes closed and his head resting lightly on the black sweater that was his fatherland. You have to have some damned fatherland, he thought. Here is mine.

"Why aren't you President?" the girl asked. "You could be an excellent president."

"Me President? I served in the Montana National Guard when I was sixteen. But I never wore a bow tie in my life and I am not, nor ever have been, an unsuccessful haberdasher. I have none of the qualifications for the Presidency. I couldn't even head the opposition even though I don't have to sit on telephone books to have my picture taken. Nor am a no-fight general. Hell, I never even was at SHAEF. I couldn't even be an elder statesman. I'm not old enough. Now we are governed in some way, by the dregs. We are governed by what you find in the bottom of dead beer glasses that whores have dunked their cigarettes in. The place has not even been swept out yet and they have an amateur pianist beating on the box."

"I don't understand it because my American is so incomplete. But it sounds awful. But don't be angry about it. Let me be angry for you."

"Do you know what an unsuccessful haberdasher is?"

"No."

"It is not discreditable. There are many of them in our country. There is at least one in every town. No, Daughter, I am only a fighting soldier and that is the lowest thing on

earth. In that you run for Arlington, if they return the
body. The family has a choice."

"Is Arlington nice?"

"I don't know," the Colonel said. "I was never buried
there."

"Where would you like to be buried?"

"Up in the hills," he said, making a quick decision. "On
any part of the high ground where we beat them."

"I suppose you should be buried on the Grappa."

"On the dead angle of any shell-pocked slope if they
would graze cattle over me in the summer time."

"Do they have cattle there?"

"Sure. They always have cattle where there is good
grass in the summer, and the girls of the highest houses,
the strong built ones, the houses *and* the girls, that resist
the snow in winter, trap foxes in the fall after they bring
the cattle down. They feed from pole-stacked hay."

"And you don't want Arlington or Père Lachaise or
what we have here?"

"Your miserable boneyard."

"I know it is the most unworthy thing about the town.
The city rather. I learned to call cities towns from you.
But I will see that you go where you wish to go and I will
go with you if you like."

"I would not like. That is the one thing we do alone.
Like going to the bathroom."

"Please do not be rough."

"I meant that I would love to have you with me. But it
is very egotistical and an ugly process."

He stopped, and thought truly, but off-key, and said, "No. You get married and have five sons and call them all Richard."

"The lion-hearted," the girl said, accepting the situation without even a glance, and playing what there was she held as you put down all the cards, having counted exactly.

"The crap-hearted," the Colonel said. "The unjust bitter criticizer who speaks badly of everyone."

"Please don't be rough in talking," the girl said. "And remember you speak worst of all about yourself. But hold me as close as we can and let's think about nothing."

He held her as close as he could and he tried to think about nothing.

CHAPTER XXX

THE Colonel and the girl lay quietly on the bed and the Colonel tried to think of nothing; as he had thought of nothing so many times in so many places. But it was no good now. It would not work any more because it was too late.

They were not Othello and Desdemona, thank God, although it was the same town and the girl was certainly better looking than the Shakespearean character, and the Colonel had fought as many, or more times than the garrulous Moor.

They are excellent soldiers, he thought. The damned Moors. But how many of them have we killed in my time? I think we killed more than a generation if you count the final Moroccan campaign against Abdel Krim. And each one you have to kill separately. Nobody ever killed them in mass, as we killed Krauts before they discovered *Einheit.*

"Daughter," he said. "Do you want me to really tell you, so you will know, if I am not rough telling it?"

"I would rather have you tell me than anything. Then we can share it."

"It cuts pretty thin for sharing," the Colonel said. "It's all yours, Daughter. And it's only the high-lights. You wouldn't understand the campaigns in detail, and few others would. Rommel might. But they always had him under wraps in France and, besides, we had destroyed his communications. The two tactical air-forces had; ours and the RAF. But I wish I could talk over certain things with him. I'd like to talk with him and with Ernst Udet."

"Just tell me what you wish and take this glass of Valpolicella and stop if it makes you feel badly. Or don't tell it at all."

"I was a spare-parts Colonel at the start," the Colonel explained carefully. "They are hang-around Colonels, which are given to a Division Commander to replace one that he may have killed, or that are relieved. Almost none are killed; but many are relieved. All the good ones are promoted. Fairly fast when the thing starts to move sort of like a forest fire."

"Go on, please. Should you take your medicine?"

"The hell with my medicine," the Colonel said. "And the hell with SHAEF."

"You explained that to me," the girl said.

"I wish the hell you were a soldier with your straight true brain and your beauty memory."

"I would wish to be a soldier if I could fight under you."

"Never fight under me," the Colonel said. "I'm cagey. But I'm not lucky. Napoleon wanted them lucky and he was right."

"We've had some luck."

"Yes," the Colonel said. "Good and bad."

"But it was all luck."

"Sure," the Colonel said. "But you can't fight on luck. It is just something that you need. The people who fought on luck are all gloriously dead like Napoleon's horse cavalry."

"Why do you hate cavalry? Almost all the good boys I know were in the three good regiments of cavalry, or in the navy."

"I don't hate anything, Daughter," the Colonel said, and drank a little of the light, dry, red wine which was as friendly as the house of your brother, if you and your brother are good friends. "I only have a point of view, arrived at after careful consideration, and an estimate of their capabilities."

"Are they not really good?"

"They are worthless," the Colonel said. Then, remembering to be kind, added, "In our time."

"Every day is a disillusion."

"No. Every day is a new and fine illusion. But you can cut out everything phony about the illusion as though you would cut it with a straight-edge razor."

"Please never cut me."

"You're not cut-able."

"Would you kiss me and hold me tight, and we both

look at the Grand Canal where the light is lovely now, and you tell me more?"

When they were looking out at the Grand Canal where the light was, indeed, lovely, the Colonel went on, "I got a regiment because the Commanding General relieved a boy that I had known since he was eighteen years old. He was not a boy any more, of course. It was too much regiment for him and it was all the regiment I ever could have hoped for in this life until I lost it." He added, "Under orders, of course."

"How do you lose a regiment?"

"When you are working around to get up on the high ground and all you would have to do is send in a flag, and they would talk it over and come out if you were right. The professionals are very intelligent and these Krauts were all professionals; not the fanatics. The phone rings and somebody calls from Corps who has his orders from Army or maybe Army Group or maybe even SHAEF, because they read the name of the town in a newspaper, possibly sent in from Spa, by a correspondent, and the order is to take it by assault. It's important because it got into the newspapers. You have to take it.

"So you leave one company dead along a draw. You lose one company complete and you destroy three others. The tanks get smacked even as fast as they could move and they could move fast both ways.

"They hit them one, two, three, four, five.

"Three men usually get out of the five (that are inside) and they run like broken-field runners that have been shaken loose in a play when you are Minnesota and the others are Beloit, Wisconsin.

"Do I bore you?"

"No. I do not understand the local allusions. But you can explain them when you care to. Please keep on telling me."

"You get into the town, and some handsome jerk puts an air mission on you. This mission might have been ordered and never cancelled. Let's give everyone the benefit of the doubt. I'm just telling you about things in a general way. It is better not to be specific and a civilian wouldn't understand it. Not even you.

"This air mission does not help much, Daughter. Because maybe you cannot stay in the town because you have got too few people in, and by now, you are digging them out of rubble; or leaving them in rubble. There are two schools of thought on that. So they say to take it by assault. They repeat this.

"This has been rigidly confirmed by some politician in uniform who has never killed in his life, except with his mouth over the telephone, or on paper, nor ever has been hit. Figure him as our next President if you want him. Figure him any way you like. But figure him and his people, the whole great business establishment, so far back that the best way to communicate with them rapidly would be by racing carrier pigeons. Except, with the amount of security they maintained for their proper persons, they would probably have their anti-aircraft shoot the pigeons down. If they could hit them.

"So you do it again. Then I will tell you what it looks like."

The Colonel looked up at the play of the light on the ceiling. It was reflected, in part, from the Canal. It made strange but steady movements, changing, as the current of a trout stream changes, but remaining, still changing as the sun moved.

Then he looked at his great beauty, with her strange, dark, grown-up child's face that broke his heart, that he would be leaving before 1335 (that was sure) and he said, "Let's not talk about the war, Daughter."

"Please," she said. "Please. Then I will have it all this week."

"That's a short sentence. I mean using the word sentence as a jail sentence."

"You don't know how long a week can be when you are nineteen."

"Several times I have known how long an hour can be," the Colonel said. "I could tell you how long two minutes and a half can be."

"Please tell me."

"Well I had two days' leave in Paris between the Schnee-Eifel fight and this one, and due to my friendship with one or two people I was privileged to be present at some sort of a meeting, where only the accredited and trusted were present, and General Walter Bedell Smith explained to all of us how easy the operation that later took the name of Hurtgen Forest would be. It was not really Hurtgen Forest. That was only a small sector. It was the Stadtswald and it was where the German High Command had figured, exactly, to fight after Aachen had been taken and the road into Germany breached. I hope I am not boring you."

"You never bore me. Nothing about fighting bores me except lies."

"You're a strange girl."

"Yes," she said. "I've known that for quite a long time."

"Would you really like to fight?"

"I don't know if I could do it. But I could try if you taught me."

"I'll never teach you. I'll just tell you anecdotes."

"Sad stories of the death of kings."

"No. GI's somebody christened them. God how I hate that word and how it was used. Comic book readers. All from some certain place. Most of them there unwillingly. Not all. But they all read a paper called 'The Stars and Stripes' and you had to get your unit into it, or you were unsuccessful as a commander. I was mostly unsuccessful. I tried to like the correspondents and there were some very good ones present at this meeting. I will not name names because I might omit some fine ones and that would be unjust. There were good ones that I don't remember. Then, there were draft dodgers, phonies who claimed they were wounded if a piece of spent metal ever touched them, people who wore the purple heart from jeep accidents, insiders, cowards, liars, thieves and telephone racers. There were a few deads missing from this briefing. They had deads too. A big percentage. But none of the deads were present as I said. They had women at it though in wonderful uniforms."

"But how did you ever marry one?"

"By mistake as I explained before."

"Go on and tell me."

"There were more maps in the room than Our Lord could read on his best day," the Colonel continued. "There were the Big Picture, the Semi-Big Picture and the Super-Big-Picture. All these people pretended to understand them, as did the boys with the pointers, a sort of half-assed billiard cue that they used for explanation."

"Don't say rough words. I don't know, even, what half-assed means."

"Shortened, or abbreviated in an inefficient manner," the Colonel explained. "Or deficient as an instrument, or in character. It's an old word. You could probably find it in Sanscrit."

"Please tell me."

"What for? Why should I perpetuate ignominy just with my mouth?"

"I'll write it if you want. I can write truly what I hear or think. I would make mistakes of course."

"You are a lucky girl if you can write truly what you hear or think. But don't you ever write one word of this."

He resumed, "The place is full of correspondents dressed according to their taste. Some are cynical and some are extremely eager.

"To ride herd on them, and to wield the pointers, there is a group of pistol-slappers. We call a pistol-slapper a non-fighting man, disguised in uniform, or you might even call it costume, who gets an erection every time the weapon slaps against his thighs. Incidentally, Daughter, the weapon, not the old pistol, the real pistol, has missed more people in combat than probably any weapon in the world. Don't ever let anyone give you one unless you want to hit people on the head with it in Harry's Bar."

"I never wanted to hit anyone; except perhaps Andrea."

"If you ever hit Andrea, hit him with the barrel; not with the butt. The butt is awfully slow, and it misses and if it lands you get blood on your hands when you put the gun away. Also please do not ever hit Andrea because he is my friend. I do not think he would be easy to hit either."

"No. I do not think so either. Please tell me some more about the meeting, or the assembly. I think I could recognize a pistol slapper now. But I would like to be checked out more thoroughly."

"Well, the pistol-slappers, in all the pride of their pistol-slappery, were awaiting the arrival of the great General who was to explain the operation.

"The correspondents were muttering, or twittering, and the intelligent ones were glum or passively cheerful. Everybody sat on folding chairs as for a Chautauqua lecture. I'm sorry about these local terms; but we are a local people.

"In comes the General. He is no pistol-slapper, but a big businessman; an excellent politician, the executive type. The Army is the biggest business, at that moment, in the world. He takes the half-assed pointer, and he shows us, with complete conviction, and without forebodings, exactly what the attack will be, why we are making it, and how facilely it will succeed. There is no problem."

"Go on," the girl said. "Please let me fill your glass and you, please look at the light on the ceiling."

"Fill it and I'll look at the light and I will go on.

"This high pressure salesman, and I say this with no disrespect, but with admiration for all his talents, or his talent, also told what we would have of the necessary. There would be no lack of anything. The organization called SHAEF was then based on a town named Versailles outside of Paris. We would attack to the east of Aachen a distance of some 380 kilometers from where they were based.

"An army can get to be huge; but you can close up a little bit. They finally went as far forward as Rheims which was 240 kilometers from the fighting. That was many months later.

"I understand the necessity of the big executive being removed from contact with his working people. I understand about the size of the army and the various problems. I even understand logistics which is not difficult. But no one ever commanded from that far back in history."

"Tell me about the town."

"I'll tell you," the Colonel said. "But I don't want to hurt you."

"You never hurt me. We are an old town and we had fighting men, always. We respect them more than all others and I hope we understand them a little. We also know they are difficult. Usually, as people, they are very boring to women."

"Do I bore you?"

"What do you think?" the girl asked.

"I bore myself, Daughter."

"I don't think you do, Richard, you would not have done something all your life if you were bored by it. Don't lie to me please, darling, when we have so little time."

"I won't."

"Don't you see you need to tell me things to purge your bitterness?"

"I know I tell them to you."

"Don't you know I want you to die with the grace of a happy death? Oh I'm getting all mixed up. Don't let me get too mixed up."

"I won't, Daughter."

"Tell me some more please and be just as bitter as you want."

CHAPTER XXXI

"LISTEN, Daughter," The Colonel said. "Now we will cut out all references to glamour and to high brass, even from Kansas, where the brass grows higher than osage-orange trees along your own road. It bears a fruit you can't eat and it is purely Kansan. Nobody but Kansans ever had anything to do with it; except maybe us who fought. We ate them every day. Osage oranges," he added. "Only we called them K Rations. They weren't bad. C Rations were bad. Ten in ones were good.

"So we fought. It is dull but it is informative. This is the way it goes if anyone is ever interested; which I doubt.

"It goes like this: 1300 Red S-3: White jumped off on time. Red said they were waiting to tie in behind White. 1305 (that is one o'clock and five minutes after in the afternoon, if you can remember that, Daughter) Blue S-3, you know what an S-3 is I hope, says, 'Let us know when you move.' Red said they were waiting to tie in behind White.

"You can see how easy it is," the Colonel told the girl. "Everybody ought to do it before breakfast."

"We cannot all be combat infantrymen," the girl told him softly. "I respect it more than anything except good, honest fliers. Please talk, I'm taking care of you."

"Good fliers are very good and should be respected as such," the Colonel said.

He looked up at the light on the ceiling and he was completely desperate at the remembrance of his loss of his battalions, and of individual people. He could never hope to have such a regiment, ever. He had not built it. He had inherited it. But, for a time, it had been his great joy. Now every second man in it was dead and the others nearly all were wounded. In the belly, the head, the feet or the hands, the neck, the back, the lucky buttocks, the unfortunate chest and the other places. Tree burst wounds hit men where they would never be wounded in open country. And all the wounded were wounded for life.

"It was a good regiment," he said. "You might even say it was a beautiful regiment until I destroyed it under other people's orders."

"But why do you have to obey them when you know better?"

"In our army you obey like a dog," the Colonel explained. "You always hope you have a good master."

"What kind of masters do you get?"

"I've only had two good ones so far. After I reached a certain level of command, many nice people, but only two good masters."

"Is that why you are not a General now? I would love it if you were a General."

"I'd love it too," the Colonel said. "But maybe not with the same intensity."

"Would you try to sleep, please, to please me?"

"Yes," the Colonel said.

"You see, I thought that if you slept you might get rid of them, just being asleep."

"Yes. Thank you very much," he said.

There was nothing to it, gentlemen. All a man need ever do is obey.

CHAPTER XXXII

"YOU slept quite well for a time," the girl told him, lovingly and gently. "Is there anything you would like me to do?"

"Nothing," the Colonel said. "Thank you."

Then he turned bad and he said, "Daughter I could sleep good straight up and down in the electric chair with my pants slit and my hair clipped. I sleep as, and when, I need it."

"I can never be like that," the girl said, sleepily. "I sleep when I am sleepy."

"You're lovely," the Colonel told her. "And you sleep better than anyone ever slept."

"I am not proud of it," the girl said, very sleepily. "It is just something that I do."

"Do it, please."

"No. Tell me very low and soft and put your bad hand in mine."

"The hell with my bad hand," the Colonel said. "Since when was it so bad."

"It's bad," the girl said. "Badder, or worse, than you will ever know. Please tell me about combat without being too brutal."

"An easy assignment," the Colonel said. "I'll skip the times. The weather is cloudy and the place is 986342. What's the situation? We are smoking the enemy with artillery and mortar. S-3 advises that S-6 wants Red to button up by 1700. S-6 wants you to button up and use plenty of artillery. White reports that they are in fair shape. S-6 informs that A company will swing around and tie in with B.

"B Company was stopped first by enemy action and stayed there of their own accord. S-6 isn't doing so good. This is unofficial. He wants more artillery but there isn't any more artillery.

"You wanted combat for what? I don't know really why. Or really know why. Who wants true combat? But here it is, Daughter, on the telephone and later I will put in the sounds and smells and anecdotes about who was killed when and where if you want them."

"I only want what you will tell me."

"I'll tell you how it was," the Colonel said, "and General Walter Bedell Smith doesn't know how it was yet. Though, probably, I am wrong, as I have been so many times."

"I'm glad we don't have to know him or the nylon-smooth man," the girl said.

"We won't have to know them this side of hell," the

Colonel assured her. "And I will have a detail guarding the gates of hell so that no such characters enter."

"You sound like Dante," she said sleepily.

"I am Mister Dante," he said. "For the moment."

And for a while he was and he drew all the circles. They were as unjust as Dante's but he drew them.

CHAPTER XXXIII

"I WILL skip the detailed part since you are, justifiably, and should be, sleepy," the Colonel said. He watched, again, the strange play of the light on the ceiling. Then he looked at the girl, who was more beautiful than any girl that he had ever seen, ever.

He had seen them come and go, and they go faster, when they go, than any other thing that flies. They can go faster from fair beauty to the knocker's shop than any other animal, he thought. But I believe that this one could hold the pace and stay the course. The dark ones last the best, he thought, and look at the bony structure in that face. This one has a fine blood line too, and she can go forever. Most of our own lovely beauties come from soda counters, and they do not know their grandfather's last name, unless, maybe, it was Schultz. Or Schlitz, he thought.

This is the wrong attitude to take, he said to himself; since he did not wish to express any of these sentiments to the girl, who would not like them anyway, and was soundly sleepy now the way a cat is when it sleeps within itself.

"Sleep well, my dearest lovely, and I will just tell it for nothing."

The girl was asleep, still holding his bad hand, that he despised, and he could feel her breathe, as the young breathe when they are easily asleep.

The Colonel told her all about it; but he did not utter it.

So after I had the privilege of hearing General Walter Bedell Smith explain the facility of the attack, we made it. There was the Big Red One, who believed their own publicity. There was the Ninth, which was a better Division than we were. There was us, who had always done it when they asked for you to do it.

We had no time to read comic books, and we had no time for practically nothing, because we always moved before first light. This is difficult and you have to throw away the Big Picture and be a division.

We wore a four-leaf clover, which meant nothing except among ourselves, who all loved it. And every time I ever see it the same thing happens in my inner guts. Some people thought that it was ivy. But it was not. It was a four-leaf clover disguised as ivy.

The orders were that we would attack with the Big Red One, the First Infantry Division of the Army of the United States, and they, and their Calypso singing PRO never let you forget it. He was a nice guy. And it was his job.

But you get fed up with horse-shit unless you like the

aroma or the taste. I never liked it. Although I loved to walk through cow-shit when I was a kid and feel it between my toes. But horse-shit bores you. It bores me very rapidly, and I can detect it at over one thousand yards.

So we attacked, the three of us in line, exactly where the Germans wished us to attack. We will not mention General Walter Bedell Smith any further. He is not the villain. He only made the promises and explained how it would go. There are no villains, I presume, in a Democracy. He was only just as wrong as hell. Period, he added in his mind.

The patches had all been removed even as far back as the rear echelon so that no Kraut would know that it was us, the three he knew so well, who were going to attack. We were going to attack with the three of us in line and nothing in reserve. I won't try to explain what that means, Daughter. But it isn't any good. And the place we were going to fight in, which I had taken a good look at, was going to be Passchendaele with tree bursts. I say that too much. But I think it too much.

The poor bloody twenty-eighth which was up on our right had been bogged down for some time and so there was pretty accurate information available about what conditions in those woods were going to be like. I think we could conservatively describe them as unfavorable.

Then we were ordered to commit one regiment before the attack started. That means that the enemy will get at least one prisoner which makes all the taking off of the Divisional patches silly. They would be waiting for us.

They would be waiting for the old four leaf clover people who would go straight to hell like a mule and do it for one hundred and five days. Figures of course mean nothing to civilians. Nor to the characters from SHAEF we never saw ever in these woods. Incidentally, and of course these occurrences are always incidental at the SHAEF level, the regiment was destroyed. It was no one's bloody fault, especially not the fault of the man who commanded it. He was a man I would be glad to spend half my time in hell with; and may yet.

It certainly would be odd if instead of going to hell, as we always counted on, we should go to one of those Kraut joints like Valhalla and not be able to get along with the people. But maybe we could get a corner table with Rommel and Udet and it would be just like any winter-sports hotel. It will probably be hell though and I don't even believe in hell.

Well anyway this regiment was rebuilt as American regiments always are by the replacement system. I won't describe it since you can always read about it in a book by somebody who was a replacement. It boils down, or distills, to the fact you stay in until you are hit badly or killed or go crazy and get section-eighted. But I guess it is logical and as good as any other, given the difficulties of transport. However it leaves a core of certain un-killed characters who know what the score is and no one of these characters liked the look of these woods much.

You could sum up their attitude in this phrase, "Don't shit me, Jack."

And since I had been an un-killed character for around

twenty-eight years I could understand their attitude. But they were soldiers, so most of them got killed in those woods and when we took the three towns that looked so innocent and were really fortresses. They were just built to tempt us and we had no word on them at all. To continue to use the silly parlance of my trade: this could or could not be faulty intelligence.

"I feel terribly about the regiment," the girl said. She had wakened and spoken straight from sleep.

"Yes," said the Colonel. "So do I. Let's drink to it once. Then you go to sleep, Daughter please. The war is over and forgotten."

Please don't think that I am conceited, Daughter, he said, without speaking. His true love was sleeping again. She slept in a different way than his career girl had slept. He did not like to remember how the career girl slept, yes he did. But he wanted to forget it. She did not sleep pretty, he thought. Not like this girl who slept as though she were awake and alive; except she was asleep. Please sleep well, he thought.

Who the hell are you to criticize career girls? he thought. What miserable career did you attempt and have failed at?

I wished to be, and was, a General Officer in the Army of the United States. I have failed and I speak badly of all who have succeeded.

Then his contrition did not last, and he said to himself, "Except the brown-nosers, the five and ten and twenty percenters and all the jerks from wherever who never fought and hold commands."

They killed several men from the academy at Gettysburg. That was the big kill day of all kill days, when there was a certain amount of opposition by both sides.

Don't be bitter. They killed General McNair by mistake the day the Valhalla Express came over. Quit being bitter. People from the Academy were killed and there are statistics to prove it.

How can I remember if I am not bitter?

Be as bitter as you want. And tell the girl, now silently, and that will not hurt her, ever, because she is sleeping so lovely. He said lovely to himself since his thinking was often ungrammatical.

CHAPTER XXXIV

SLEEP softly, my true love, and when you wake, this will be over and I will joke you out of trying to learn details of the *triste métier* of war and we will go to buy the little negro, or moor, carved in ebony with his fine features, and his jeweled turban. Then you will pin him on, and we will go to have a drink at Harry's and see whoever or whatever of our friends that will be afoot at that hour.

We will lunch at Harry's, or we'll come back here, and I will be packed. We will say good-bye and I will get into the *motoscafo* with Jackson, and make some cheerful crack to the *Gran Maestro* and wave to any other members of the Order, and ten to one, the way I feel right now, or two will get you thirty, we will not ever see one another again.

Hell, he said to no one, and certainly not aloud, I've felt this way before many fights and almost always at some time in the fall of the year, and always when leaving Paris. Probably it doesn't mean a thing.

Who gives a damn anyway except me and the *Gran Maestro* and this girl; I mean at command level.

I give very much of a damn myself. But I certainly should be trained and adjusted by this time not to give a muck for nothing; like the definition of a whore. A woman who does not etc.

But we won't think about that boy, lieutenant, captain, major, colonel, general sir. We will just lay it on the line once more and the hell with it, and with its ugly face that old Hieronymus Bosch really painted. But you can sheathe your scythe, old brother death, if you have got a sheath for it. Or, he added, thinking of Hurtgen now, you can take your scythe and stick it up your ass.

It was Passchendaele with tree bursts, he told nobody except the wonder light on the ceiling. Then he looked at the girl, to see that she was sleeping well enough so even his thoughts would not hurt her.

Then he looked at the portrait and he thought, I have her in two positions, lying down, turned a little on her side, and looking at me straight in front. I'm a lucky son of a bitch and I should never be sad about anything.

CHAPTER XXXV

THE first day there, we lost the three battalion commanders. One killed in the first twenty minutes and the other two hit later. This is only a statistic to a journalist. But good battalion commanders have never yet grown on trees; not even Christmas trees which was the basic tree of that woods. I do not know how many times we lost company commanders how many times over. But I could look it up.

They aren't made, nor grown, as fast as a crop of potatoes is either. We got a certain amount of replacements but I can remember thinking that it would be simpler, and more effective, to shoot them in the area where they detrucked, than to have to try to bring them back from where they would be killed and bury them. It takes men to bring them back, and gasoline, and men to bury them. These men might just as well be fighting and get killed too.

There was snow, or something, rain or fog, all the time

and the roads had been mined as many as fourteen mines deep in certain stretches, so when the vehicles churned down to a new string deeper, in another part of the mud, you were always losing vehicles and, of course, the people that went with them.

Besides just mortaring it all to hell and having all the fire-lanes taped for machine gun, and automatic weapon fire, they had the whole thing worked out and canalized so however you out-thought them you ran right into it. They also shelled you with heavy artillery fire and with at least one railway gun.

It was a place where it was extremely difficult for a man to stay alive even if all he did was be there. And we were attacking all the time, and every day.

Let's not think about it. The hell with it. Maybe two things I will think about and get rid of them. One was a bare-assed piece of hill that you had to cross to get into Grosshau.

Just before you had to make this run, which was under observation with fire by 88's, there was a little piece of dead ground where they could only hit you with a how-itzer, only interdicting fires, or, from the right by mortar. When we cleaned it up we found they had good observation for their mortars there too.

This was a comparatively safe place, I'm really not lying, not me nor anybody else. You can't fool those that were in Hurtgen, and if you lied they would know it the minute you opened your mouth, Colonel or no Colonel.

We met a truck at this place and slowed up, and he had

the usual gray face and he said, "Sir, there is a dead GI in the middle of the road up ahead, and every time any vehicle goes through they have to run over him, and I'm afraid it is making a bad impression on the troops."

"We'll get him off the road."

So we got him off the road.

And I can remember just how he felt, lifting him, and how he had been flattened and the strangeness of his flatness.

Then there was one other thing, I remember. We had put an awful lot of white phosphorus on the town before we got in for good, or whatever you would call it. That was the first time I ever saw a German dog eating a roasted German kraut. Later on I saw a cat working on him too. It was a hungry cat, quite nice looking, basically. You wouldn't think a good German cat would eat a good German soldier, would you Daughter? Or a good German dog eat a good German soldier's ass which had been roasted by white phosphorus.

How many could you tell like that? Plenty, and what good would they do? You could tell a thousand and they would not prevent war. People would say we are not fighting the krauts and besides the cat did not eat me nor my brother Gordon, because he was in the Pacific. Maybe land crabs ate Gordon. Or maybe he just deliquesced.

In Hurtgen they just froze up hard; and it was so cold they froze up with ruddy faces. Very strange. They all were gray and yellow like wax-works, in the summer. But once the winter really came they had ruddy faces.

Real soldiers never tell any one what their own dead looked like, he told the portrait. And I'm through with this whole subject. And what about that company dead up the draw? What about them, professional soldier?

They're dead, he said. And I can hang and rattle.

Now who would join me in a glass of Valpolicella? What time do you think I should wake your opposite number, you girl? We have to get to that jewelry place. And I look forward to making jokes and to talking of the most cheerful things.

What's cheerful, portrait? You ought to know. You're smarter than I am, although you haven't been around as much.

All right, canvas girl, the Colonel told her, not saying it aloud, we'll drop the whole thing and in eleven minutes I will wake the live girl up, and we will go out on the town, and be cheerful and leave you here to be wrapped.

I didn't mean to be rude. I was just joking roughly. I don't wish to be rude ever because I will be living with you from now on. I hope, he added, and drank a glass of the wine.

CHAPTER XXXVI

IT was a sharp, cold bright day, and they stood outside
the window of the jeweler's shop and studied the two
small negro heads and torsos that were carved in ebony and
adorned with studded jewels. One was as good as the other,
the Colonel thought.

"Which do you like the best, Daughter?"

"I think the one on the right. Don't you think he has the
nicer face?"

"They both have nice faces. But I think I would rather
have him attend you if it was the old days."

"Good. We'll take him. Let's go in and see them. I must
ask the price."

"I will go in."

"No, let me ask the price. They will charge me less than
they would charge you. After all you are a rich American."

"Et toi, Rimbaud?"

"You'd make an awfully funny Verlaine," the girl told
him. "We'll be some other famous characters."

"Go on in, Majesty, and we'll buy the god damn jewel."

"You wouldn't make a very good Louis Sixteenth either."

"I'd get up in that tumbril with you and still be able to spit."

"Let's forget all the tumbrils and everyone's sorrows, and buy the small object and then we can walk to Cipriani's and be famous people."

Inside the shop they looked at the two heads and she asked the price, and then, there was some very rapid talk and the price was much lower. But still it was more money than the Colonel had.

"I'll go to Cipriani's and get some money."

"No," the girl said. Then to the clerk, "Put it in a box and send it to Cipriani's and say the Colonel said to pay for it and hold it for him."

"Please," the clerk said. "Exactly as you say."

They went out into the street and the sunlight and the unremitting wind.

"By the way," the Colonel said. "Your stones are in the safe at the Gritti in your name."

"Your stones."

"No," he told her, not rough, but to make her understand truly. "There are some things that a person cannot do. You know about that. You cannot marry me and I understand that, although I do not approve it."

"Very well," the girl said. "I understand. But would you take one for a lucky stone?"

"No. I couldn't. They are too valuable."

"But the portrait has value."

"That is different."

"Yes," she agreed. "I suppose so. I think I begin to understand."

"I would accept a horse from you, if I was poor and young, and riding very well. But I could not take a motor-car."

"I understand it now very well. Where can we go now, at this minute, where you can kiss me?"

"In this side alley, if you know no one who lives in it."

"I don't care who lives in it. I want to feel you hold me tight and kiss me."

They turned into the side street and walked toward its blind end.

"Oh, Richard," she said. "Oh, my dear."

"I love you."

"Please love me."

"I do."

The wind had blown her hair up and around his neck and he kissed her once more with it beating silkily against both his cheeks.

Then she broke away, suddenly, and hard, and looked at him, and said, "I suppose we had better go to Harry's."

"I suppose so. Do you want to play historical personages?"

"Yes," she said. "Let us play that you are you and I am me."

"Let's play," the Colonel said.

CHAPTER XXXVII

THERE was no one in Harry's except some early morning drinkers that the Colonel did not know, and two men that were doing business at the back of the bar.

There were hours at Harry's when it filled with the people that you knew, with the same rushing regularity as the tide coming in at Mont St. Michel. Except, the Colonel thought, the hours of the tides change each day with the moon, and the hours at Harry's are as the Greenwich Meridian, or the standard meter in Paris, or the good opinion the French military hold of themselves.

"Do you know any of these morning drinkers?" he asked the girl.

"No. I am not a morning drinker so I have never met them."

"They will be swept out when the tide comes in."

"No. They will leave, just as it comes, of their own accord."

"Do you mind being here out of season?"

"Did you think I was a snob because I come from an old family? We're the ones who are not snobs. The snobs are what you call jerks, and the people with all the new money. Did you ever see so much new money?"

"Yes," the Colonel said. "I saw it in Kansas City when I used to come in from Ft. Riley to play polo at the Country Club."

"Was it as bad as here?"

"No, it was quite pleasant. I liked it and that part of Kansas City is very beautiful."

"Is it really? I wish that we could go there. Do they have the camps there too? The ones that we are going to stay at?"

"Surely. But we'll stay at the Muehlebach hotel which has the biggest beds in the world and we'll pretend that we are oil millionaires."

"Where will we leave the Cadillac?"

"Is it a Cadillac now?"

"Yes. Unless you want to take the big Buick Roadmaster, with the Dynaflow drive. I've driven it all over Europe. It was in that last Vogue you sent me."

"We'd probably better just use one at a time," the Colonel said. "Whichever one we decide to use we will park in the garage alongside the Muehlebach."

"Is the Muehlebach very splendid?"

"Wonderful. You'll love it. When we leave town we'll drive north to St. Joe and have a drink in the bar at the Roubidoux, maybe two drinks, and then we will cross the river and go west. You can drive, and we can spell each other."

"What is that?"

"Take turns driving."

"I'm driving now."

"Let's skip the dull part and get to Chimney Rock and go on to Scott's Bluff and Torrington and after that you will begin to see it."

"I have the road maps and the guides and that man who says where to eat, and the A.A.A. guide to the camps and the hotels."

"Do you work on this much?"

"I work at it in the evenings, with the things you sent me. What kind of a license will we have?"

"Missouri. We'll buy the car in Kansas City. We fly to Kansas City, don't you remember? Or we can go on a really good train."

"I thought we flew to Albuquerque."

"That was another time."

"Will we stop early in the afternoons at the best Motel in the A.A.A. book and I make you any drinks you want while you read the paper and Life and Time and Newsweek, and I will read the new fresh Vogue and Harper's Bazaar?"

"Yes. But we come back here too."

"Of course. With our car. On an Italian liner; whichever one is best then. We drive straight here from Genova."

"You don't want to stop anywhere for the night?"

"Why? We want to get home to our own house."

"Where will our house be?"

"We can decide that any time. There are always plenty of houses in this town. Would you like to live in the country too?"

"Yes," the Colonel said. "Why not?"

"Then we could see the trees when we woke up. What sort of trees will we see on this journey?"

"Pine mostly, and cotton-wood along the creeks, and aspen. Wait till you see the aspen turn yellow in the fall."

"I'm waiting. Where will we stay in Wyoming?"

"We'll go to Sheridan first and then decide."

"Is Sheridan nice?"

"It's wonderful. In the car we'll drive to where they had the Wagon-Box Fight and I'll tell you about it. We will drive up, on the way to Billings, to where they killed that fool George Armstrong Custer, and you can see the markers where everybody died and I'll explain the fight to you."

"That will be wonderful. Which is Sheridan more like, Mantova or Verona or Vicenza?"

"It isn't like any of those. It is right up against the mountains, almost like Schio."

"Is it like Cortina then?"

"Nothing like. Cortina is in a high valley in the mountains. Sheridan lays right up against them. They aren't any foot-hills to the Big Horns. They rise high out of the plateau. You can see Cloud's Peak."

"Will our cars climb them properly?"

"You're damn right they will. But I would much rather not have any hydromatic drive."

"I can do without it," the girl said. Then she held herself straight and hard not to cry. "As I can do without everything else."

"What are you drinking?" the Colonel said. "We haven't even ordered yet."

"I don't think I will drink anything."

"Two very dry Martinis," the Colonel said to the bartender, "and a glass of cold water."

He reached into his pocket and unscrewed the top of the medicine bottle, and shook two of the big tablets into his left hand. With them in his hand, he screwed the top back on the bottle. It was no feat for a man with a bad right hand.

"I said I didn't want to drink anything."

"I know daughter. But I thought you might need one. We can leave it on the bar. Or I can drink it myself. Please," he said. "I did not mean to be brusque."

"We haven't asked for the little negro that will look after me."

"No. Because I did not want to ask for him until Cipriani came in and I could pay for him."

"Is everything that rigid?"

"With me, I guess," the Colonel said. "I'm sorry daughter."

"Say daughter three times straight."

"Hija, figlia, Daughter."

"I don't know," she said. "I think we should just leave

here. I love to have people see us, but I don't want to see anybody."

"The box with the negro in it is on top of the cash register."

"I know. I've seen it for sometime."

The bar-tender came, with the two drinks, frost cold from the chilled coldness of the glasses, and he brought the glass of water.

"Give me that small packet that came in my name and is on top of the cash register," the Colonel said to him. "Tell Cipriani I will send him a check for it."

He had made another decision.

"Do you want your drink, daughter?"

"Yes. If you don't mind me changing my mind too."

They drank, after touching the glasses very lightly, so lightly that the contact was almost imperceptible.

"You were right," she said feeling its warmth and its momentary destruction of sorrow.

"You were right too," he said and palmed the two tablets.

He thought taking them with the water now was in bad taste. So, when the girl turned her head a moment to watch a morning drinker go out the door, he swallowed them with the Martini.

"Should we go, Daughter?"

"Yes. By all means."

"Bar-tender," the Colonel said. "How much are these drinks? And do not forget to tell Cipriani I am sending him a check for this nonsense."

CHAPTER XXXVIII

THEY ate lunch at the Gritti, and the girl had unwrapped the small ebony negro's head and torso, and pinned it high on her left shoulder. It was about three inches long, and was quite lovely to look at if you liked that sort of thing. And if you don't you are stupid, the Colonel thought.

But do not even think rough, he told himself. You have to be good now in every way until you say good-bye. What a word, he thought, good-bye.

It sounds like a Valentine slogan.

Good-bye and *bonne chance* and *hasta la vista*. We always just said *merde* and let it go at that. Farewell, he thought, that is a nice word. It sings well, he thought. Farewell, a long farewell and take it with you where you go. With handles, he thought.

"Daughter," he said. "How long has it been since I told you that I loved you?"

"Not since we sat at the table."

"I tell you now."

She had combed her hair with patience when they came into the hotel and she had gone into the room for women. She disliked such rooms.

She had used lipstick to make the sort of mouth she knew he most desired, and she had said to herself, making the mouth correctly, "Don't think at all. Don't think. Above all don't be sad because he is going now."

"You look beautiful."

"Thank you. I would like to be beautiful for you if I could and if I could be beautiful."

"Italian is a lovely language."

"Yes. Mister Dante thought so."

"*Gran Maestro*," the Colonel said. "What is there to eat in this *Wirtschaft*?"

The *Gran Maestro* had been observing, without observing, with affection and without envy.

"Do you want meat, or fish?"

"It's Saturday," the Colonel said. "Fish is not compulsory. So I'll take it."

"It is sole," the *Gran Maestro* said. "What do you want, my Lady?"

"Whatever you decide. You know more about food than I do, and I like it all."

"Make a decision, Daughter."

"No. I would rather leave it to some one who knows more than me. I have a boarding school appetite."

"It will come as a surprise," the *Gran Maestro* said with

his long and loving face with the grey eyebrows over the softly hooded eyes, and the ever happy face of the old soldier who is still alive and appreciates it.

"Is there any news from the Order?" the Colonel asked.

"Only that our leader, Himself, is in trouble. They have confiscated everything he owns. Or at any rate they have intervened."

"I hope it is not serious."

"We will have confidence in our leader. He has ridden out worse tempests than this."

"To our leader," the Colonel said.

He raised his glass, which had been filled with the decanted new and true Valpolicella. "Drink to him, daughter."

"I can't drink to that swine," the girl said. "Besides I do not belong to the Order."

"You are a member now," the *Gran Maestro* said. "*Por merito di guerra.*"

"I'll drink to him then," she said. "Am I really a member of the Order?"

"Yes," the *Gran Maestro* said. "You have not received your parchment yet but I appoint you Super Honorary Secretary. My Colonel will reveal to you the secrets of the order. Reveal, please, my Colonel."

"I reveal," the Colonel said. "There are no pitted folk about?"

"No. He is out with his Lady. Miss Baedeker."

"OK then," the Colonel said. "I will reveal. There is only

270

the major secret that you must know. Correct me, *Gran Maestro*, if I fall into error."

"Proceed to reveal," the *Gran Maestro* said.

"I proceed to reveal," the Colonel said. "Listen carefully daughter. This is the Supreme Secret. Listen. 'Love is love and fun is fun. But it is always so quiet when the gold fish die.'"

"It has been revealed," the *Gran Maestro* said.

"I am very proud and happy to be a member of the Order," the girl said. "But it is, in a way, a rather rough order."

"It is indeed," the Colonel said. "And now, *Gran Maestro*, what do we actually eat; without mysteries?"

"Some crab *enchillada*, in the style of this town, but cold, first. Served in the shell. Then sole for you, and for my lady a mixed grill. What vegetables?"

"Whatever you have," the Colonel said.

The *Gran Maestro* was gone and the Colonel looked at the girl and then at the Grand Canal outside the window, and he saw the magic spots and changes of light that were even here, in the end of the bar, which had now by skillful handling been made into a dining room, and he said, "Did I tell you, daughter, that I love you?"

"You haven't told me for quite a long time. But I love you."

"What happens to people that love each other?"

"I suppose they have whatever they have, and they are more fortunate than others. Then one of them gets the emptiness forever."

"I won't be rough," the Colonel said. "I could have made a rough response. But please don't have any emptiness."

"I'll try," the girl said. "I've been trying ever since I woke up. I've tried ever since we knew each other."

"Keep on trying, daughter," the Colonel said.

Then to the *Gran Maestro*, who had reappeared, having given his orders, the Colonel said, "A bottle of that *vino secco*, from Vesuvius, for the small soles. We have the Valpolicella for the other things."

"Can't I drink the Vesuvius wine with my mixed grill?" the girl asked.

"Renata, daughter," the Colonel said. "Of course. You can do anything."

"I like to drink the same wines as you if I drink wine."

"Good white wine is good with a mixed grill, at your age," the Colonel told her.

"I wish there was not such a difference in ages."

"I like it very much," the Colonel said. "Except," he added. Then he did not continue and said, "Let's be *fraîche et rose comme au jour de bataille*."

"Who said that?"

"I haven't the slightest idea. I picked it up when I took a course at the *Collége des Maréchaux*. A rather pretentious title. But I graduated. What I know best I learned from the krauts, studying them and opposing them. They are the best soldiers. But they always over-reach."

"Let's be like you said, and please tell me that you love me."

"I love you," he said. "That's what you can base on. I tell you truly."

"It is Saturday," she said. "And when is next Saturday?"

"Next Saturday is a movable feast, daughter. Find me a man who can tell me about next Saturday."

"You could tell me if you would."

"I'll ask the *Gran Maestro*, maybe he knows. *Gran Maestro* when will next Saturday come?"

"*A Pâques ou à la Trinité*," the *Gran Maestro* said.

"Why don't we have any smells from the kitchen to cheer us up?"

"Because the wind is from the wrong direction."

Yes, the Colonel thought. The wind is from the wrong direction and how lucky I would have been to have had this girl instead of the woman that I pay alimony to, who could not even make a child. She hired out for that. But who should criticise whose tubes? I only criticize Goodrich or Firestone or General.

Keep it clean, he said to himself. And love your girl.

She was there beside him, wishing to be loved, if he had any love to give.

It came back, as it always had, when he saw her, and he said, "How are you with the crow wing hair and the breakheart face?"

"I'm fine."

"*Gran Maestro*," the Colonel said. "Produce a few smells or something from your off-stage kitchen, even if the wind is against us."

CHAPTER XXXIX

THE hall porter had telephoned, under the direction of the concierge, and it was the same motor boat that they had ridden in before.

T 5 Jackson was in the boat with the luggage, and the portrait, which had been well and sturdily wrapped. It was still blowing hard.

The Colonel had paid his bill and made the proper tips. The people of the hotel had put the luggage and the picture in the boat, and seen that Jackson was seated properly. Then they had retired.

"Well, daughter," the Colonel said.

"Can't I ride with you to the garage?"

"It would be just as bad at the garage."

"Please let me ride to the garage."

"All right," the Colonel said. "It's your show, really. Get in."

They did not talk at all, and the wind was a stern wind

so that, with what speed the old calamity of a motor made, there seemed almost to be no wind at all.

At the landing place, where Jackson was handing the luggage to a porter, and looking after the portrait himself, the Colonel said, "Do you want to say good-bye here?"

"Do I have to?"

"No."

"May I come up to the bar in the garage while they are getting the car down?"

"That will be worse."

"I do not care."

"Get that stuff up to the garage, and have somebody look after it until you get the car down," the Colonel said to Jackson. "Check on my guns and pack this stuff in a way to give the maximum space in the rear seat."

"Yes, sir," Jackson said.

"Am I going then?" the girl asked.

"No," the Colonel told her.

"Why can't I go?"

"You know very well. You weren't invited."

"Please don't be bad."

"Christ, Daughter, if you knew how hard I am trying not to be. It's easy if you're bad. Let's pay this good man off, and go over and sit on the bench there under the tree."

He paid the owner of the motor boat, and told him that he had not forgotten about the jeep engine. He also told him not to count on it, but that there was a good chance that he could get it.

"It will be a used engine. But it will be better than that coffee pot you have in there now."

They went up the worn stone steps and walked across the gravel and sat on a bench under the trees.

The trees were black and moved in the wind, and there were no leaves on them. The leaves had fallen early, that year, and been swept up long ago.

A man came over to offer postcards for sale and the Colonel told him, "Run along, son. We don't need you now."

The girl was crying, finally, although she had made the decision never to cry.

"Look, Daughter," the Colonel said. "There isn't anything to say. They didn't install shock-absorbers in this vehicle we ride in now."

"I've stopped," she said. "I'm not an hysterical."

"I wouldn't say you were. I'd say you were the loveliest and most beautiful girl that ever lived. Any time. Any place. Anywhere."

"If it were true, what difference would it make?"

"You have me there," the Colonel said. "But it is true."

"So now what?"

"So now we stand up and kiss each other and say good-bye."

"What's that?"

"I don't know," the Colonel said. "I guess that is one of the things everybody has to figure out for themselves."

"I'll try to figure it."

"Just take it as easy as you can, Daughter."

"Yes," the girl said. "In the vehicle without the shock-absorbers."

"You were tumbril bait from the start."

"Can't you do anything kindly?"

"I guess not. But I've tried "

"Please keep on trying. That's all the hope we have."

"I'll keep on trying."

So they held each other close and kissed each other hard and true, and the Colonel took the girl across the stretch of gravel and down the stone steps.

"You ought to take a good one. Not that old displaced engine boat."

"I'd rather take the displaced engine boat if you don't mind."

"Mind?" the Colonel said. "Not me. I only give orders and obey orders. I don't mind. Good-bye, my dear, lovely, beautiful."

"Good-bye," she said.

CHAPTER XL

HE was in the sunken oak hogshead that they used in the Veneto for blinds. A blind is any artifice you use to hide the shooter from that which he is attempting to shoot, which, in this case, were ducks.

It had been a good trip out with the boys, once they had met in the garage, and a good evening with excellent food cooked on the old open-hearth kitchen. Three shooters rode in the rear seat, on the way to the shooting place. Those who did not lie had permitted themselves a certain amount of exaggeration and the liars had never been in fuller flower.

A liar, in full flower, the Colonel had thought, is as beautiful as cherry trees, or apple trees when they are in blossom. Who should ever discourage a liar, he thought, unless he is giving you co-ordinates?

The Colonel had collected liars all his life, as some men gather postage-stamps. He did not classify them, except at

278

the moment, nor treasure them truly. He just enjoyed, completely, hearing them lie at the moment, unless, of course, something concerned with duty was involved. Last night there had been a fair amount of good lying after the grappa had been passed around, and the Colonel had enjoyed it.

There had been smoke in the room from the open charcoal fire; no, there were logs, he thought. Anyway a liar lies best when there is a little smoke or when the sun has set.

He had come close to lying twice himself, and had held it up, and merely exaggerated. I hope anyway, he thought.

Now here was the frozen lagoon to ruin everything. But it was not ruined.

A pair of pin-tails came, suddenly, from nowhere, slanting down fast in a dive no airplane ever made, and the Colonel heard their feathered trajectory and swung and killed the drake. He lay on the ice, hitting it as solid as a duck can hit ice, and, before he was down, the Colonel had killed his mate, who was climbing, long-necked and fast.

She fell alongside the drake.

So it is murder, the Colonel thought. And what isn't nowadays? But, boy, you can still shoot.

Boy, hell, he thought. You beat-up old bastard. But look at them come now.

They were widgeon, and they came in a whisp that coagulated and then stretched to nothing. Then they coagulated again and the treacherous duck on the ice started to talk to them.

Let them turn once more, the Colonel said to himself. Keep your head down, and do not move even your eyes. They are going to come in.

They came in well, with treachery speaking to them.

Their wings were suddenly set to alight, as when you lower the flaps. Then they saw it was ice and they rose, climbing.

The shooter, who was not a Colonel now, nor anything but a gun handler, rose in the wooden barrel and got two. They hit the ice almost as solidly as the big ducks.

Two is enough from one family, the Colonel said. Or was it one tribe?

The Colonel heard a shot behind him, where he knew there was no other blind, and turned his head to look across the frozen lagoon to the far, sedge-lined shore.

That does it, he thought.

A bunch of mallards, that had been coming in low, were flaring up into the sky, seeming to stand on their tails as they climbed.

He saw one fall, then heard another shot.

It was the sullen boatman shooting at the ducks that would have come to the Colonel.

How, how can he do that? the Colonel thought.

The man had a shot-gun to shoot any cripples that might be escaping where the dog could not get them. For him to fire at ducks that were coming to the Colonel's blind was, in shooting, as bad a thing as one man could do to another.

The boatman was too far away to hear a shout. So the Colonel fired at him twice.

It is too far for the pellets to reach, he thought, but at least he will know that I know what he is doing. What the hell is this all about? On a beautifully run shoot like this one too? This is the best organized and best run duck shoot I have ever shot at and I have had as much fun shooting here as I ever had in my life. What is the matter with that son of a bitch?

He knew how bad his anger was for him. So he took two of the pills and washed them down with a drink of Gordon's gin from his flask since there was no water.

He knew the gin was bad for him too and he thought, everything is bad for me except rest and very light exercise. OK, rest and light exercise, boy. Do you suppose that is light exercise?

You, beauty, he said to himself. I wish you were here now and we were in the double blind and if we could only just feel the backs of our shoulders touch. I'd look around and see you and I would shoot the high ducks well, to show off and try to put one in the blind without having it hit you. I'd try to pull one down like this, he said, hearing the wings in the air. He rose, turned, saw the single drake, long necked and beautiful, the wings fast moving and travelling to the sea. He saw him sharp and clear and in the sky with the mountains behind him. He met him, covered him and pulled as he swung as far back as he could swing the gun.

The drake came down on the ice, just outside the

perimeter of the blind, and broke the ice as he fell. It was the ice that had been broken to put out the decoys and it had re-frozen lightly. The calling hen looked at him as he lay and shifted her feet.

"You never saw him before in your life," the Colonel said to the hen. "I don't believe you even saw him coming. Though you may have. But you didn't say anything."

The drake had hit with his head down and his head was under the ice. But the Colonel could see the beautiful winter plumage on his breast and wings.

I'd like to give her a vest made of the whole plumage the way the old Mexicans used to ornament their gods, he thought. But I suppose these ducks have to go to the market and no one would know how to skin and cure the skins anyway. It could be beautiful, though, with Mallard drake skins for the back and sprig for the front with two longitudinal stripes of teal. One coming down over each breast. Be a hell of a vest. I'm pretty sure she'd like it.

I wish that they would fly, the Colonel thought. A few fool ducks might come in. I have to stay ready for them if they do. But none came in and he had to think.

There were no shots from the other blinds and only occasional shots from the sea.

With the good light, the birds could see the ice and they no longer came in and instead went out to the open sea to raft up. So he had no shooting and he thought without intention, trying to find what had made it at the first. He knew he did not deserve it and he accepted it and he lived by it, but he sought, always, to understand it.

One time it had been two sailors when he had been walking with the girl at night. They had whistled at her and, the Colonel thought, that was a harmless enough thing and he should have let it go.

But there was something wrong with it. He sensed it before he knew it. Then he knew it solidly, because he had stopped under a light, in order that they might see what he wore on his shoulders, so that they might take the other side of the street.

What he wore on each shoulder was a small eagle with wings out-stretched. It was embroidered onto the coat he wore in silver thread. It was not conspicuous, and it had been there a long time. But it was visible.

The two sailors whistled again.

"Stay over there against the wall if you want to watch it," the Colonel had said to the girl. "Or look away."

"They are very big and young."

"They won't be big for long," the Colonel promised her.

The Colonel walked over to the whistlers.

"Where is your shore patrol?" he asked.

"How would I know?" the biggest whistler said. "All I want is a good look at the dame."

"Do people like you have names and serial numbers?"

"How would I know," one said.

The other said, "I wouldn't tell a chicken Colonel if I had."

Old army boy, the Colonel thought, before he hit him. Sea lawyer. Knows all his rights.

But he hit him with a left from nowhere and hit him three times as he started to go.

The other one, the first whistler, had closed fast and well, for a man who had been drinking, and the Colonel gave him the elbow in the mouth and then, under the light, had a good right hand shot at him. When it was in, he glanced at the second whistler and saw that was okay.

Then he threw a left hook. Then he put the right way into the body, coming up. He threw another left hook and then turned away and walked toward the girl because he did not want to hear the head hit the pavement.

He checked on the one that had it first, and noted he slept peacefully, chin down, with the blood coming out of his mouth. But it was still the right color, the Colonel noted.

"Well, there goes my career," he said to the girl. "Whatever that was. But those people certainly wear funny pants."

"How are you?" the girl asked.

"I'm fine. Did you watch it?"

"Yes."

"I'll have bad hands in the morning," he said absentmindedly. "But I think we can walk away from it all right. But let's walk slowly."

"Please walk slowly."

"I did not mean it that way. I meant let's not be hurried in our departure."

"We will walk as slowly as two people can walk."

So they walked.

"Do you want to try an experiment?"

"Of course."

"Let's walk so we make even the backs of our legs look dangerous."

"I'll try. But I don't think I can."

"Well, let's just walk then."

"But didn't they hit you?"

"One pretty good right behind the ear. The second boy when he came in."

"Is that what fighting's like?"

"When you're lucky."

"And when you're not lucky?"

"Your knees bend too. Either forward or backward."

"Do you still care for me after you have fought?"

"I love you much more than before if it were possible."

"Can't it be possible? It would be nice. I love you more since I saw that thing. Am I walking slowly enough?"

"You walk like a deer in the forest, and sometimes you walk as well as a wolf, or an old, big coyote when he is not hurried."

"I'm not sure I wish to be an old big coyote."

"Wait till you see one," the Colonel said. "You'll wish. You walk like all the great predators, when they walk softly. And you are not a predator."

"That I can promise."

"Walk a little ahead so I can see."

She walked ahead and the Colonel said, "You walk like a champion before he is the champion. If you were a horse I would buy you if I had to borrow the money at twenty percent a month."

"You don't have to buy me."

"I know about that. That was not what we were discussing. We were discussing your gait."

"Tell me," she said. "What happens to those men? That's one of the things I don't know about fighting. Shouldn't I have stayed and cared for them?"

"Never," the Colonel told her. "Remember that; never. I hope they split a good concussion between them. They can rot. They caused the accident. There is no question of civil responsibility. We were all insured. If I can tell you one thing, Renata, about fighting."

"Tell me please."

"If you ever fight, then you must win it. That's all that counts. All the rest is cabbage, as my old friend Dr. Rommel put it."

"Did you really like Rommel?"

"Very much."

"But he was your enemy."

"I love my enemies, sometimes, more than my friends. And the Navy, you know, wins all their fights always. This I learned in a place called the Pentagon building when I was still permitted to enter that building by the front door. If you like we can stroll back down this street, or walk it fast, and ask those two that question."

"I tell you truly, Richard. I have seen enough fighting for one night."

"Me too, to tell the truth," the Colonel said. But he said it in Italian and it started, "*Anche io*. Let's go to Harry's for one, and then I will walk you home."

"Didn't you hurt your bad hand?"

"No," he explained. "I only threw it once to the head. The other times I punched to the body with it."

"May I feel it?"

"If you will feel very softly."

"But it is terribly swollen."

"There is nothing broken in it and that sort of swelling always goes down."

"Do you love me?"

"Yes. I love you with two moderately swollen hands and all my heart."

CHAPTER XLI

SO that was that, and maybe it was that day or maybe
it was another that made the miracle. You never knew,
he thought. There was the great miracle and he had never
consciously implemented it. Nor, he thought, you son of a
bitch, did you ever oppose it.

It was colder than ever and the broken ice re-froze and
the calling duck did not even look up now. She had aban-
doned treachery for an attempt at security.

You bitch, the Colonel thought. Though that is unjust.
It is your trade. But why is it a hen calls better than a drake.
You ought to know, he thought. And even that's not true.
What the hell is true? Drakes actually call better.

Now don't think of her. Don't think of Renata because
it won't do you any good, boy. It might even be bad for
you. Also you said good-bye. What a good-bye that was.
Complete with tumbrils. And she would have climbed up
in the damned tumbril with you too. Just so long as it was

a real tumbril. Very rough trade, he thought. Loving and leaving. People can get hurt at it.

Who gave you a right to know a girl like that?

Nobody, he answered. But Andrea introduced me to her.

But how could she love a sad son of a bitch like you?

I do not know, he thought truly. I truly do not know.

He did not know, among other things, that the girl loved him because he had never been sad one waking morning of his life; attack or no attack. He had experienced anguish and sorrow. But he had never been sad in the morning.

They make almost none like that, and the girl, although she was a young girl, knew one when she saw one.

Now she is at home and sleeping, the Colonel thought. That is where she ought to be and not in any god damn duck blind with the decoys frozen up on us.

I wish to hell she was here though, if this were a double blind, and have her looking to the west just in case one string did come in. It would be nice if she were warm enough. Maybe I can trade somebody out of one of these real down jackets that nobody ever sold that had one. The kind they issued to the Air Force once by mistake.

I could find out how they are quilted and make one with duck down from here, he thought. I'd get a good tailor to cut it and we would make it double-breasted with no pocket on the right and lay in a chamois shooting patch so the gun butt would never catch.

I'll do it, he said to himself. I'll do it, or I will get one off some joker and have it cut down for her. I'd like to get her a good Purdey 12, not too damn light, or a pair of Boss over and unders. She should have guns as good as she is. I suppose a pair of Purdey's, he thought.

Just then he heard the light swish of pinions, fast beating in the air, and looked up. But they were too high. He only looked up with his eyes. But they were so high they could see the barrel, and him in it, and the frozen-in decoys with the dejected hen, who saw them too, and quacked hard in her loyal treachery. The ducks, they were pintails, continued on their flight out toward the sea.

I never give her anything, as she pointed out. There was the small moor's head. But it does not mean anything. She selected it and I bought it. That is no way to give a gift.

What I would like to give her is security, which does not exist anymore; all my love, which is worthless; all my worldly goods, which are practically non-existent except for two good shot-guns, my soldier suits, the medals and decorations with the citations, and some books. Also a retired Colonel's pay.

With all my worldly goods I thee endow, he thought.

And she gave me her love, some hard stones, which I returned, and the picture. Well, I can always give her back the picture. I could give her my ring from V.M.I., he thought, but where the hell did I lose that?

She wouldn't want a D.S.C. with cluster, nor two silver stars, nor the other junk, nor the medals of her own country. Nor those of France. Nor those of Belgium. Nor the trick ones. That would be morbid.

I better just give her my love. But how the hell do you send it? And how do you keep it fresh? They can't pack it in dry ice.

Maybe they can. I must inquire. But how do I get that condemned jeep engine to that old man?

Figure it out, he thought. Figuring things out has been your trade. Figuring things out when they were shooting at you, he added.

I wish that son of a bitch that is lousing up the duck shooting had a rifle and I had a rifle. We would find out pretty soon who could figure things out. Even in a lousy barrel in a marsh where you can't maneuver. He'd have to come to get me.

Stop that, he said to himself, and think about your girl. You do not want to kill anyone anymore; ever.

Who are you feeding that to, he told himself. You going to run as a Christian? You might give it an honest try. She would like you better that way. Or would she? I don't know, he said frankly. I honest to Christ don't know.

Maybe I will get Christian toward the end. Yes, he said, maybe you will. Who wants to make a bet on that?

"You want to bet on that?" he asked the calling duck. But she was looking up at the sky behind him and had commenced her small chuckling talk.

They came over too high and never circled. They only looked down and went on toward the open sea.

They must really be rafted up out there, the Colonel

thought. There's probably some punt gunner trying to sneak up on them now. They will be pretty close into the lee with the wind and someone is sneaking onto them now surely. Well, when he makes his shot some may break back this way. But with it frozen-up I suppose I really ought to pull out instead of staying here like a fool.

I have killed enough and I have shot as well or better than I can shoot. Better hell, he thought. Nobody shoots better than you here except Alvarito and he's a kid and shoots faster. But you kill fewer ducks than many bad and fair shots.

Yes, I know about that. I know about that and why and we don't go by the numbers anymore and we threw away the book too, remember?

He remembered how, by some miracle of chance in a war, he had been with his best friend for a moment in action in the Ardennes and they were pursuing.

It was early fall and it was on a high upland with sandy roads and trails and the trees were scrub oak and pines. The enemy tank and half track prints showed clearly in the moist sand.

It had rained the day before, but now it was clearing and visibility was good and you could see well across all the high, rolling country and he and his friend were glassing it as carefully as though they were hunting game.

The Colonel, who was a General then, and an assistant divisional commander, knew the individual print of each tracked vehicle they were pursuing. He also knew when the enemy vehicles had run out of mines and approximately the number of rounds that remained to them. He also had figured where they had to fight before they reached the Siegfried. He was sure they would not fight at either of these two places but would race for where they were going.

"We're pretty far up for people of our exalted rank, George," he said to his best friend.

"Ahead of the point, General."

"It's okay," the Colonel had said. "Now we throw away the book and chase for keeps."

"I couldn't agree more fully, General. Because I wrote the book myself," his best friend said. "But suppose they had left something there?"

He pointed to the logical place to defend.

"They didn't leave anything there," the Colonel had said. "They haven't enough stuff left even for a chickenshit fire-fight."

"Everybody's right until he's wrong," his best friend said, adding, "General."

"I'm right," the Colonel said. He was right, too, although in obtaining his exact knowledge he had not fulfilled the complete spirit of the Geneva Convention which was alleged to govern the operation of war.

"Let's really chase," his best friend had said.

"There's nothing holding us up and I guarantee they won't stop at either of those two. I didn't get that from any kraut either. That's from my head."

He looked over the country once more, and heard the wind in the trees and smelled the heather under their boots and looked once more at the tracks in the wet sand and that was the end of that story.

I wonder if she'd like that? he thought. No. It builds me up too much. I'd like to get somebody else to tell it to her though and build me solid. George can't tell it to her. He's the only one that could tell it to her and he can't. He sure as hell can't.

I've been right over ninety-five percent of the time and that's a hell of a batting average even in something as simple as war. But that five percent when you are wrong can certainly be something.

I'll never tell you about that, Daughter. That's just a noise heard off stage in my heart. My lousy chicken heart. That bastard heart certainly couldn't hold the pace.

Maybe he will, he thought, and took two of the tablets and a swallow of gin and looked across the gray ice.

I'm going to get that sullen character in now and pick up and get the hell to the farm house or the lodge, I suppose that I should call it. The shooting's over.

CHAPTER XLII

THE COLONEL had signalled the boatman in by standing up, in the sunken barrel, firing two shots toward the empty sky, and then waving him toward the blind.

The boat came in slowly, breaking ice all the way, and the man picked up the wooden decoys, caught the calling hen and put her in her sack, and, with the dog slithering on the ice, picked up the ducks. The boatman's anger seemed to be gone and to be replaced by a solid satisfaction.

"You shot very few," he said to the Colonel.

"With your help."

That was all they said and the boatman placed the ducks carefully, breasts up, on the bow of the boat and the Colonel handed his guns and the combination cartridge box and shooting stool into the boat.

The Colonel got into the boat and the boatman checked the blind and unhooked the pocketed, apron-like device which had hung on the inside of the blind to hold shells. Then he got into the boat too and they commenced their slow and laborious progress out through the ice to the open water of the brown canal. The Colonel worked as hard with the poling oar as he had worked coming in. But now, in the bright sunlight, with the snow mountains to the north, and the line of the sedge that marked the canal ahead of them, they worked together in complete co-ordination.

Then they were into the canal, slipping breakingly in from the last ice; then, suddenly, light-borne and the Colonel handed the big oar to the boatman and sat down. He was sweating.

The dog, who had been shivering at the Colonel's feet, pawed his way over the gunwale of the boat and swam to the canal bank. Shaking the water from his white be-draggled coat, he was into the brown sedge and brush, and the Colonel watched his progress toward home by the movement of the brush. He had never received his sausage.

The Colonel, feeling himself sweating, although he knew he was protected from the wind by his field jacket, took two tablets from the bottle and a sip of gin from his flask.

The flask was flat and of silver with a leather cover. Under the leather cover, which was worn and stained, it was engraved, on one side, to Richard From Renata With Love. No one had ever seen this inscription except the girl, the Colonel, and the man who had engraved it. It had not been engraved in the same place it was purchased. That was in the earliest days, the Colonel thought. Now who cared?

On the screw-on top of the flask was engraved From R. to R.C.

The Colonel offered the flask to the boatman who looked at him, at the flask, and said, "What is it?"

"English grappa."

"I'll try it."

He took a long drink of it; the type of drink peasants take from a flask.

"Thank you."

"Did you have good shooting?"

"I killed four ducks. The dog found three cripples shot by other people."

"Why did you shoot?"

"I'm sorry that I shot. I shot in anger."

I have done that myself sometimes, the Colonel thought, and did not ask him what the anger was about.

"I am sorry they did not fly better."

"Shit," the Colonel said. "That's the way things go."

The Colonel was watching the movement the dog made in the high grass and sedge. Suddenly he saw him stop; he was quite still. Then he pounced. It was a high leap and a dive forward and down.

"He has a cripple," he said to the boatman.

"Bobby," the boatman called. "Bring. Bring."

The sedge moved and the dog came out with a mallard drake in his jaws. The gray white neck and the green head were swaying up and down as a snake's might move. It was a movement without hope.

The boatman put the boat in sharp for shore.

"I'll take him," the Colonel said. "Bobby!"

He took the duck from the dog's light-holding mouth and felt him intact and sound and beautiful to hold, and with his heart beating and his captured, hopeless eyes.

He looked at him carefully, gentling him as you might gentle a horse.

"He's only wing-tipped," he said. "We'll keep him for a caller or to turn loose in the Spring. Here, take him and put him in the sack with the hen."

The boatman took him carefully and put him in the burlap bag that was under the bow. The Colonel heard the hen speak to him. Or, maybe she is protesting, he thought. He could not understand duck-talk through a burlap bag.

"Take a shot of this," he said to the boatman. "It's damned cold today."

The boatman took the flask and drank deeply again.

"Thank you," he said. "Your grappa is very, very good."

CHAPTER XLIII

AT the landing, before the long low stone house by the side of the canal, there were ducks laid out on the ground in rows.

They were laid in groups that were never of the same number. There were a few platoons, no companies, and, the Colonel thought, I barely have a squad.

The head game-keeper was standing on the bank in his high boots, his short jacket and his pushed back old felt hat, and he looked critically at the number of ducks on the bow of the boat as they came alongshore.

"It was frozen-up at our post," the Colonel said.

"I suspected so," the head keeper said. "I'm sorry. It was supposed to be the best post."

"Who was top gun?"

"The Barone killed forty-two. There was a little current there that kept it open for a while. You probably did not hear the shooting because it was against the wind."

"Where is everyone?"

"They're all gone except the Barone who is waiting for you. Your driver is asleep in the house."

"He would be," the Colonel said.

"Spread those out properly," the head keeper told the boatman who was a game-keeper too. "I want to put them in the game book."

"There is one green-head drake in the bag who is only wing-tipped."

"Good. I will take good care of him."

"I will go inside and see the Barone. I'll see you later."

"You must get warm," the head keeper said. "It's been a bitter day, my Colonel."

The Colonel started to walk toward the door of the house.

"I'll see you later," he said to the boatman.

"Yes, my Colonel," the boatman said.

Alvarito, the Barone, was standing by the open fire in the middle of the room. He smiled his shy smile and said in his low pitched voice, "I am sorry you did not have better shooting."

"We froze up completely. I enjoyed what there was very much."

"Are you very cold?"

"Not too cold."

"We can have something to eat."

"Thank you. I'm not hungry. Have you eaten?"

"Yes. The others went on and I let them take my car.

Can you give me a lift to Latisana or just above? I can get transportation from there."

"Of course."

"It was a shame that it should freeze. The prospects were so good."

"There must have been a world of ducks outside."

"Yes. But now they won't stay with their feed frozen over. They will be on their way south tonight."

"Will they all go?"

"All except our local ducks that breed here. They'll stay as long as there is any open water."

"I'm sorry for the shoot."

"I'm sorry you came so far for so few ducks."

"I always love the shoot," the Colonel said. "And I love Venice."

The Barone Alvarito looked away and spread his hands toward the fire. "Yes," he said. "We all love Venice. Perhaps you do the best of all."

The Colonel made no small talk on this but said, "I love Venice as you know."

"Yes. I know," the Barone said. He looked at nothing. Then he said, "We must wake your driver."

"Has he eaten?"

"Eaten and slept and eaten and slept. He has also read a little in some illustrated books he brought with him."

"Comic books," the Colonel said.

"I should learn to read them," the Barone said. He smiled the shy, dark smile. "Could you get me some from Trieste?"

"Any amount," the Colonel told him. "From superman on up into the improbable. Read some for me. Look, Alvarito, what was the matter with that game-keeper who poled my boat? He seemed to have a hatred for me at the start. Pretty well through, too."

"It was the old battle-jacket. Allied uniform affects him that way. You see he was a bit over-liberated."

"Go on."

"When the Moroccans came through here they raped both his wife and his daughter."

"I think I'd better have a drink," the Colonel said.

"There is grappa there on the table."

CHAPTER XLIV

THEY had dropped the Barone off at a villa with great gates, a gravelled drive and a house, which, since it was over six miles from any military objective, had the good fortune not to have been bombed.

The Colonel had said good-bye and Alvarito had told him to come down and shoot any, or every, week-end.

"You're sure you won't come in?"

"No. I must get back to Trieste. Will you give my love to Renata?"

"I will. Is that her portrait that you have wrapped in the back of the car?"

"It is."

"I'll tell her that you shot very well and that the portrait was in good condition."

"Also my love."

"Also your love."

"*Ciao*, Alvarito, and thank you very much."

"*Ciao*, my Colonel. If one can say *ciao* to a Colonel."

"Consider me not a Colonel."

"It is very difficult. Good-bye, my Colonel."

"In case of any unforeseen contingencies would you ask her to have the portrait picked up at the Gritti?"

"Yes, my Colonel."

"That's all, I guess."

"Good-bye, my Colonel."

CHAPTER XLV

THEY were out on the road now and the early darkness was beginning.

"Turn left," the Colonel said.

"That's not the road for Trieste, sir," Jackson said.

"The hell with the road to Trieste. I ordered you to
turn left. Do you think there is only one way in the world
to get to Trieste?"

"No, sir. I was only pointing out to the Colonel—"

"Don't you point me out a God-damn thing and until
I direct you otherwise, don't speak to me until you are
spoken to."

"Yes, sir."

"I'm sorry, Jackson. What I mean is I know where I'm
going and I want to think."

"Yes, sir."

They were on the old road that he knew so well and
the Colonel thought, well, I sent four of the ducks I

promised to those I promised them to at the Gritti. There wasn't enough shooting to be enough feathers to do that boy's wife any good with feathers. But they are all big ducks and fat and they will be good eating. I forgot to give Bobby the sausage.

There was no time to write Renata a note. But what could I say, in a note, that we did not say?

He reached into his pocket and found a pad and pencil. He put on the map reading light, and with his bad hand, printed a short message in block letters.

"Put that in your pocket, Jackson, and act on it if necessary. If the circumstances described occur, it is an order."

"Yes, sir," Jackson said and took the folded order blank with one hand and put it in the top left hand pocket of his tunic.

Now take it easy, the Colonel said to himself. Any further concern you may have is about yourself and that is just a luxury.

You are no longer of any real use to the Army of the United States. That has been made quite clear.

You have said good-bye to your girl and she has said good-bye to you.

That is certainly simple.

You shot well and Alvarito understands. That is that.

So what the hell do you have to worry about, boy? I hope you're not the type of jerk who worries about what happens to him when there's nothing to be done. Let's certainly hope not.

Just then it hit him as he had known it would since they had picked up the decoys.

Three strikes is out, he thought, and they gave me four. I've always been a lucky son of a bitch.

It hit him again, badly.

"Jackson," he said. "Do you know what General Thomas J. Jackson said on one occasion? On the occasion of his unfortunate death. I memorized it once. I can't respond for its accuracy of course. But this is how it was reported: 'Order A. P. Hill to prepare for action.' Then some more delirious crap. Then he said, 'No, no, let us cross over the river and rest under the shade of the trees.' "

"That's very interesting, sir," Jackson said. "That must have been Stonewall Jackson, sir."

The Colonel started to speak but he stopped while it hit him the third time and gripped him so he knew he could not live.

"Jackson," the Colonel said. "Pull up at the side of the road and cut to your parking lights. Do you know the way to Trieste from here?"

"Yes, sir, I have my map."

"Good. I'm now going to get into the large back seat of this god-damned, over-sized luxurious automobile."

That was the last thing the Colonel ever said. But he made the back seat all right and he shut the door. He shut it carefully and well.

After a while Jackson drove the car down the ditch and willow lined road with the car's big lights on, looking for a place to turn. He found one, finally, and turned carefully. When he was on the right-hand side of the road, facing south toward the road juncture that would put him on the highway that led to Trieste, the one he was familiar with, he put his map light on and took out the order blank and read:

IN THE EVENT OF MY DEATH THE WRAPPED PAINTING AND THE TWO SHOTGUNS IN THIS CAR WILL BE RETURNED TO THE HOTEL GRITTI VENICE WHERE THEY WILL BE CLAIMED BY THEIR RIGHTFUL OWNER SIGNED RICHARD CANTWELL, COL., INFANTRY, U.S.A.

"They'll return them all right, through channels," Jackson thought, and put the car in gear.